T0374443

CROOKED

THOMAS VENTERS

CROOKED

iUniverse books may be ordered through booksellers or by contacting:

iUniverse
1663 Liberty Drive
Bloomington, IN 47403
www.iuniverse.com
1-800-Authors (1-800-288-4677)

ISBN: 978-1-5320-7133-1 (sc)
ISBN: 978-1-5320-7134-8 (e)

Library of Congress Control Number: 2019903564

Print information available on the last page.

iUniverse rev. date: 04/02/2019

ONE

HOMERUN

"What a great way to end the day," Myles proclaimed as he bent down to observe the decapitated head below him. Beside him was the first responding police officer on the scene.

"Yup," the officer sighed. "The little old lady next door heard screaming, so she called 911. She says it was the most gut-wrenching sound she's ever heard in her long life."

"How long ago was the call?" Myles asked the officer.

"Around 15 minutes ago. 10:10ish."

"Do we have anyone patrolling the streets in case the suspect is still around?"

"Yeah," the officer nodded. "Hayden was in the area, so he's patrolling until we can get more officers down here."

Myles stood up and walked over to the living room as another detective inspected the lifeless body. Myles recognized the detective as his friend Karter: the ginger, slightly flamboyant, blue-eyed FBI agent wearing his

1

navy blue jacket with the yellow "FBI" letters marked across the front and back.

"Hey Autumn." Myles grinned as Karter stood up.

"Ugh, why do you guys still call me that?" Karter looked like a midget only being 5'3 next to his much taller associate.

"Let's not get a'head' of ourselves here. There's no 'knee'd to get hasty." Myles tried concealing his laughter, but Karter couldn't help it.

Their snickering came to a halt though as they heard another investigator enter the house through the back door. The voice came from none other than Sergeant Williams. His dark toned arms seemed to be torturing his short-sleeved shirt sleeves, and his face sported an unkempt stubble. "October 4th," he articulated as he wrote on a notepad. "2091; homicide of a young white male... Have we identified the victim?" he asked Karter.

"Jonathan Martly. Age: 36. Shattered right patella... Head has received blunt force trauma to the frontal bone... Head has been severed at the base of the skull... slits in the palm of the right hand."

The officer listened in from the bedroom where the head was, which was across the kitchen on the other side of the house from the living room. "What's a patella..?"

"It's the kneecap," Myles answered as he turned towards the back door in the kitchen. "I'll be right back. I'm going to see if I can gather any more information on the victim."

Myles ducked down as he left the house so he wouldn't hit his head. Unlike Karter's height, Myles was 7 foot tall. He walked to the front yard past the yellow police tape, blinded by the flashing blue and red lights emitting from the dozens of cop cars. A freezing breeze of cold California air came past Myles as he opened his car door, giving him goosebumps.

"Alright... Jonathan Martly..." Myles pulled up documents about the victim on his mobile data terminal. He didn't seem to be a friend with the law. Many gang-related crimes including smuggling drugs and guns. They believed he was part of a small gang called the '*Aesthetics*;' he was simply a carrier for them.

As Myles looked for more insight on the victim, all hell seemed to break loose outside. Police swarmed the front lawn of the house, as more officers appeared, handling their business confidently. Inside the house, Karter inspected the scene with a camera and some kind of measurement.

"The water faucet is still on..." Karter observed, pacing the floor as he spoke to Sergeant Williams. "Some dishes are clean, and others are still dirty. This would imply that he was in the middle of washing dishes when something happened. It was so sudden, he didn't have enough time to turn it off."

"Maybe that's when he saw the suspect?" Sergeant Williams inferred.

"That is a possibility," Karter agreed. "All three locks on the front door are locked, and there's no sign of entry through any windows, in fact, they're locked as well. Backdoor was wide open according to the first responding officer. I'm pretty sure the suspect entered and exited through the back door."

Williams rubbed his chin. "The sink is to the right to the back door though, and the living room is to the left of the back door. If the suspect entered through the back door, how is it that the victim ended up in the living room?"

Karter shrugged as he took a picture of the shattered glass table in the living room. "Not sure. Maybe there was a weapon in the living room or in the next room that he thought he could defend himself with. Maybe he was dragged. Maybe he knew the suspect."

"Did you find the murder weapon yet?" Sargent Williams asked.

"Not yet. We think there are likely two murder weapons. Something sharp enough to cut a head off, and something blunt enough to shatter a kneecap." Karter then took a picture of the headless body. Only then did he notice through the flash in the camera the shine of a massive shard of glass. "The glass from the table seems very robust; I bet there are no more than a dozen shards here. I'd say a body fell and shattered it. I don't know about you, but that heavy glass shard doesn't seem like it would just fly across the room if someone fell on it. I don't think it's a coincidence that it's next to the body either."

Williams' eyebrow raised "You think the suspect cut off the victims head with the glass?"

"That's what it looks like." Karter then bent down to the body and looked at where the head was severed. "The cut doesn't look clean like what you'd see from a knife. It's ridged and dull…" Karter was then taken back by something, so he got a closer look.

"What is it?" Sergeant Williams inquired. He watched as Karter reached into the esophagus with a gloved hand, pulling out something black.

"It's a… It's a pawn." Karter stood up. "Looks like

we have a signature here. Typical work of a planned assassination."

Myles returned, bearing a pencil and paper with him. "Suspect seems to be a troublemaker. My guess is that this is gang-related violence." Myles started sketching the scene onto the paper.

Karter was still taking pictures. "There's a 9 mil in the bedroom along with some coke. No weapons in the living room or the room next to it. If the suspect came through the back door, the logical thing to do would be to run for the gun in the bedroom and kill the suspect, but he didn't."

"Unless the murderer was in the bedroom to begin with," Myles input.

"Maybe he knew the victim had a weapon in the bedroom," William stated.

Karter shook his head. "If that were the case, that would mean that the killer did surveillance for who knows how long."

"Maybe he knew the victim," Williams interjected. "You did say that this murder was planned right? An assassination."

Myles bent down to the body, affirming what he knew. "The suspect was hit in the frontal part of the skull, and the Kneecap. Both are knocking blows to the anterior part of the body, supporting the evidence that he was coerced into the living room."

"So we know that either of those blows would lead to the victim falling over onto the table, shattering it." Williams turned over to the glass shard on the ground next to the body. "Once it was shattered, he had to of been dragged off the glass so that the suspect could grab the glass shard."

Karter rubbed his cheek as he kept the thought going. "There was definitely some struggle then… Meaning the victim was alive as the suspect cut his head off…"

"Which means he was more likely to have been hit in the knee before his head was decapitated," Myles asserted. "Maybe as soon as he pulled his head off, he hit it across the room with the blunt object to the wall; must've hit a home run. That's when he ran, leaving the door wide open."

Karter's seemed to look uncomfortable as Myles explained his theory. "Well, that just about explains it… Let's finish up on sketching the scene; then we can start looking for evidence."

TWO
RECRUIT

Investigating a crime scene can be a tedious process, which Myles was well aware of. It requires a lot of careful handling of evidence and information. Through experience in the past, Myles knew that the difficulty of a case would be solely based on human error. Luckily for the suspect, there wasn't a lot the detectives could find at the scene. Nothing completely obvious that is.

Myles sat in a lab by himself carefully going through what they could find. He originally majored in microbiology, but always had a knack for justice. He eventually found a great deal at the Zone Law Enforcement Agency, or the ZLEA for short. Back in 2050, parts of the US decided to set up what they called "zones" or regions in highly populated areas where crime rates were higher on average. These zones were much like districts but mostly correlated with the police; occupied by officers with as much training as the FBI. The specific zone he worked in was the PCPD or Palm City Police Department; Region O4337-82.

Myles had worked for the PCPD for 6 years now and

was very satisfied with what they offered to him. They had a side by side program that supported both of his interests. Being a 22-year-old, he took that opportunity immediately. The only drawback was that there was a lot of work involved; nonetheless, he loved it all. He could be in a lab one day, then solving a murder mystery the next. The academy he went to had living quarters where he could sleep, but he preferred sleeping in the apartments across town. This meant that he didn't get much sleep at all after what happened the night before.

Myles heard someone come into the lab behind him just as he was testing the blood samples that were found at the scene. He was delighted to see that it was his longtime partner in crime, Hayden. He was an average man; green eyes, short dark brown hair; average height, and a scar on the right side of his head.

"Find anything yet?" Hayden asked as he put his hands into his pants pockets.

"Not really," Myles sighed. "Whoever the suspect is, they definitely are good at covering their tracks. I do have something little though." Myles pointed to a table that had shattered glass from the crime scene. They were all put together like a puzzle. Myles made sure to point out one little shard that was missing. "They looked everywhere, but nothing was found."

Hayden appeared to be slightly unamused by this discovery. "And? I don't see where you're going with this."

"We are starting to believe that the victim grabbed that shard of glass and stabbed the suspect with it. Maybe somewhere on the leg. That's why the victim's right palm is sliced up. The suspect got aggravated and smashed his head with the bat; ran off with the glass shard in his leg so we didn't get any traces of his blood."

Hayden didn't seem too convinced. "There would have to be some point that blood would drip out, right?"

"That's why I'm going through the blood samples." Myles looked over to the table with the breathable containers filled with dark red blood. "It all had to happen fast though. The handiwork is sloppy. By the time the suspect got to the last bit of tissue on the neck, he simply ripped it off. He only had around 10 minutes to do all of this, and cutting the head off of a live human is very difficult. This is why we think he was hit in the head before this period; conscious, but disoriented. Once he pulled the head off, he ran for the door, but not before tossing the head at the bedroom wall across the kitchen."

Hayden had a look of influence. "I would have never guessed. Seems like you put it all together. You always did have a mind for puzzles."

Myles smiled before turning back to his work.

Myles and Hayden met each other as far back as when they both applied for ZLEA. They helped each other when they needed it, which is why their bond started very early in their friendship. Hayden was one of the rare people to see Myles truly smile, and not out of sarcasm. Myles wasn't exactly the most welcoming detective on the force, but he couldn't help the fact that he looked so intimidating. His eyes were sharp as if they could stab straight through with one glimpse; the color was a deep shade of ocean blue. He looked as though he was able to stare straight into his victim's soul. It always looked like he was mad or irritated, but in reality, he was feeling completely normal. He had what was to referred to as "pissy resting face."

In the lab, Myles always kept his hair back either behind his ear or in a ponytail; as to not contaminate anything. As for his lab coat, he'd wear it inside and outside of the laboratory. It made for a great jacket at times like these.

"Hey, I think Anderson needs you," Hayden stated. "He sent me down here to get you. Something about a new officer here."

Myles felt a little impatient by the sudden interruption in his work. "When does he need me?"

"As soon as possible he said. How much do you want to bet he wants you to give a newbie a tour of the academy?"

"I hope to god not." Myles took his disposable rubber gloves off as he led Hayden out of the lab. "I'll see you later then. Wish me luck."

"Later." Hayden waved.

PCPD was home to many officers who knew what they were doing. It was closed off by gates that surrounded the campus and had numerous features that a college would have. That's because this place was prepared to educate students if they felt that they qualified as an important asset. PCPD was one of many zones in the surrounding cities; ran by three main directors. Anderson happened to be the one in charge of the police force itself. The others were in charge of different aspects such as money handling, recruiting, and educating.

Anderson was no doubt one of the most intimidating people on the force for new recruits. Myles, however, knew him before he became a director. Ever since then, Myles had set a personal goal to climb that ranked ladder in the force.

PCPD was divided into sections based on specific qualities that tie them together. There was a building for handling evidence; adjacent to which would be the offices where officers would work. Finding this structure was no difficulty – it was the main building – seven stories high with a parking lot connected directly to it. Anderson's office was on the seventh floor; the floor that housed only the highest ranked officials for PCPD. Myles looked across the campus from the elevator window as it went up. He watched as guys and girls walked with their backpacks from wing to wing in order to reach their class on time. It reminded him of his days back in college when he used to have friends he'd go out with every other weekend. The feeling of nostalgia filled his mind as he took in a deep breath of air; preparing himself for what was to come once he reached Anderson's office.

"Come take a seat," Anderson directed in a deep voice. Anderson's office always emanated an aroma of new leather furniture. Compared to the other offices on the lower floors, this almost seemed like a room in a mansion. Anderson sat at a dark wooden table in a leather seat. Behind him stood a kid who didn't look anything over 20. "Myles Connor, meet Cooper Alcorn. Cooper Alcorn, meet Myles Connor." Anderson paused to allow Myles and Cooper to shake hands before continuing. "This will be your new partner."

Myles' eyes opened wide. "With all due respect sir... I have a very difficult case that may redirect my focus elsewhere..."

Anderson sat back in his chair and interlocked his fingers. "That's why you're going to help him. The kid is very studious. High grades; knows the ups and downs. The only problem is that he lacks real first-hand experience. He's already gotten experience as a cop and wants to get into detective work and you are well equipped for the job. You are required to have an apprentice for a full year before becoming the rank above what you are now. If you refuse, you will not receive the promotion."

Myles shifted in his chair uncomfortably before looking up to Cooper, then back to Anderson. "Yes, sir..."

Anderson smiled in delight. "Great. Every week, I expect to receive an evaluation report on all that he has accomplished." Cooper looked nervous by the way his instructor was behaving.

The way down to Myles' office was silent. Myles was irritated as usual as Cooper followed from behind like a puppy. His hair was light brown, shaven on the sides and back. The top was combed over to the side, which made it seem well kept except for the curled hair astray from the rest going down his forehead. He had green eyes and a slight butt chin. His height though was comparable to Karter.

"So partner, first thing's what?" His Australian accent was strong and recognizable.

"Paperwork," Myles said bluntly as he entered his office. "Get used to these four walls. You'll be seeing it 80% of the time you work here for the next year."

Cooper seemed intimidated for sure, but he wanted

to find a way to prove himself. "Better than the offices on the second floor! That's for sure!"

The reaction on Myles' face made him back down, though that wasn't Myles' intention. "See the stack of papers over on that filing cabinet? It'd be great help if you could sort those out for me. Consider it your first accomplishment on your evaluation."

THREE

DECAY

Karter never liked working alone; he would much rather work alongside someone he could trust. This was supposed to be a simple procedure though. The first thing Karter wanted to do was question the people that Jonathan Martly knew. The database made it clear that he was in the gang 'Aesthetics,' but it's never easy to point out the top dog. Instead, Karter tried pinpointing someone that wasn't as hard to find but was well aware of who Jonathan was. This just so happened to be another fellow gang member named Erik Vincent, who they believed to be the one getting profit from smuggling. Jonathan was just the carrier; Erik was the one with the goods.

When going in to question someone, there are a lot of things an officer must consider. They'll need to have exactly what they need to ask written down; as for the answers to the questions. A competent agent will always research more about the person they are interrogating to expect what's to be expected.

Karter's car was unmarked, meaning his car didn't

have numbers or colors or even the name 'police' on it. The most he had was lights and sirens. As he pulled up to Erik's house, he made sure to scan the area to know who was watching if anyone was doing so at all. This was an important lesson Karter had learned when in the force. It was in the middle of the afternoon, so it was easier to tell if someone could be watching. As he got out, he made sure to check for his equipment. He usually carried around a gun, which seemed to have been influenced by the old and primitive Glock, and some handcuffs in a pouch on his belt; all of which had been concealed to the naked eye. The most important thing he had, which he tried not to hide, was his FBI badge hung from around his neck.

As Karter walked up to the house, he placed his right hand on his sidearm in case there was sudden trouble that'd turn into a gunfight. He knocked on the door four times with the bottom of his fist. A moment of silence passed before Karter tried again, this time stating his department.

"FBI! Open up!" he yelled to whoever was inside.

The house didn't include a garage, and there wasn't a car so Karter was sure Erik wasn't home at this time. He decided to check through the windows in case he saw a light or TV on. From what he could tell, no one was home. He felt awkward standing around in a neighborhood like this; it was not a place that welcomed law enforcement.

Karter knew Erik had a warehouse not too far from where he lived. It was marked down as a warehouse full of taxidermy, but the police were certain it was just a place where Erik could stash his cash and other illegal acts. As he pulled up into the parking lot, he saw a car that he identified as Erik's vehicle. After checking the license plates, he confirmed he was here. This was exceptionally fortunate since it was alone, so he didn't expect company.

Getting out of his car, Karter felt chills go down his spine; something made him feel uneasy. The sky was losing its light, turning into a darker shade of blue, and the walls of the warehouse had graffiti he couldn't decipher the meaning to. Karter put a hand on his sidearm as he banged four times on the door.

"FBI!" Karter repeated several times before giving up.

He tried opening the door, but to no surprise, it was locked. As he looked around the building, he found that all doors were locked, windows were boarded up, and even the overhead doors wouldn't budge. Karter didn't know what to do, yet he knew Erik had to be in there somewhere.

Karter walked around the building, discovering what seemed to be a back entryway. It was a considerably large warehouse, so Karter was afraid Erik didn't hear him. The back door was on the second-floor balcony, accessed by stairs which extended to them. As Karter climbed the rusty and underkept stairs, he started to question whether or not he made the right decision by not calling back up. Working on the force for so long, Karter started to feel invincible when going through dangerous situations. This cockiness could be the reason for his reckless moments. The balcony itself seemed rusty and structurally weak, though that didn't stop him from trying to find a way in or to at least get the attention of Erik. His sudden determination turned into terror as part of the scaffolding caved in, and Karter fell into the building, landing on a goat that he then ruined.

The metal from the scaffolding cut up his leg, but the adrenaline from falling made him more worried about Erik getting the impression someone was breaking in.

"FBI! Make yourself known!" he screamed as he pulled his sidearm out and pointed it into the darkness.

Karter soon smelt something lingering in the air... It was a smell he recognized very well from his past investigations. The smell brought bad memories to his thoughts. It was the distinctive smell of rotting flesh. There was no obvious way out, and Karter's instincts turned to survival mode. Being in a dark room, Karter expected to see the worse as he clicked the flashlight to his Glock on.

"FBI! Make yourself known or I will shoot!" Karter screamed as he looked around the room, seeing dozens of taxidermy animals looking at him with their glass eyes.

Karter could feel his heart rate get faster; his demeanor changed from confident to fearful. He could almost feel his eyes welling up from the state of his condition. He took heavy breaths as he scanned the room carefully; just as he did in training. It was almost like a nightmare; being surrounded by stuffed animals with the lingering smell of death. In survival situations, the human body will envision the worst possible scenario, especially if it doesn't fully understand what's going on.

The air he breathed choked him, and every shadow made from the taxidermy made Karter's skin crawl. He cleared out each room, checking for anything actually living before entering. He was afraid that if anyone was in the warehouse, they could hear his heart beating up from his throat through the eerie silence. Walking passed a room, he kicked something which startled him. It was some sort of rattling of what sounded like empty brass shells on the ground. Looking closer, he realized that they were empty bullet casings for a gun, meaning that somewhere nearby, there could be a gun. Near the bullet casings was some sort of black residue, which created a trail. Karter decided to follow it, not knowing where it might lead him.

As he ventured farther into the warehouse, the rotten smell became more potent, until Karter reached the final room. The transition into this room was hot and humid, and the smell made Karter gag. As he shined his light down the room, the hairs on the back of his neck stood up, and his face went pale. Adrenaline shot up through his veins, and he instantly had the instinct to run. There was something so frightening about seeing a stuffed human standing straight up, and staring at the entrance for the next beholder to witness.

FOUR

FIRE

Myles took a long puff of his cigarette, looking out from his car window. He held his breath for a few seconds before blowing out a cloud of smoke.

"Williams said he should be here somewhere," Myles stated.

Next to Myles in the passenger seat was Cooper, looking out for a short, pudgy, African American male named Mike Robertson. Mike was allegedly the one to run his mouth about the aesthetics if he needed to. He was the one that would settle agreements, and bring information to the gang. After some surveillance Williams made after a few short days, he determined a pattern he could follow.

"Keep your eyes peeled," Sergeant Williams stressed. "It's 8:30. He should be around here any minute now."

Cooper grabbed the mic off of the radio and pressed the output button. "Over, Sergeant Williams. I repeat Ov—"

"Gimme that," Myles demanded, interrupting Cooper as he grabbed the microphone from his hand.

"Did I do something wrong?" Cooper asked.

"No, you're just so… new," Myles shook his head.

"How would he have known if we heard the order or not though?" Cooper inquired.

"It's okay if you show that you heard him by saying 'copy,' but don't go around saying 'over' and 'I repeat' like how the movies do it."

Cooper looked down, taking note of the tip. Myles then nudged him, spotting someone that fit the description of who they were looking for. He reached for the mic on the UHF. "You think that's our guy?"

Williams' voice came over the receiver. "It could be. Let's go and check."

Myles looked over to Cooper as he spoke into the radio. "Copy," he overemphasized.

Myles got out of the car, making his way to the sidewalk. Cooper was nearest to the sidewalk, so he led. As they got near the man, he started to look suspicious; Cooper spoke first.

"Are you Mike Robertson?" Cooper inquired.

"N-no… my name is… Chuck… Johnson…" the man stuttered.

Cooper crumbled, turning around to Myles. "Damn… isn't our guy…"

Myles walked pass Cooper. "Don't be so naïve." Now speaking to the man, Myles continued "Chuck Johnson huh? Are you aware that there's a street named after you?"

"There is..?" the man questioned nervously.

"Yes. In fact, I believe it's this street we're on right now."

"Ah man!" the man acted surprised. "That's so cool! What a coincidence!"

By this time Sergeant Williams moved in behind the man and spoke in a deep voice. "Let me see some ID," he demanded.

The man turned to Williams suddenly. "I... left it at home."

Myles could see the man was obviously Mike. He didn't appear to be the type of person that would be in a gang though; Myles had met far more dangerous criminals than Mike before. "Alright then. Well until we know for sure, I can detain you."

"Says who!" Mike protested.

"Says the investigation we're on!" Myles argued. "Listen, we're here on the case of a murder. Maybe you'd know about it. Jonathan Martly was murdered, and we're trying to catch the one who did this."

Mike seemed to be more calm about the situation by that point, but still reluctant.

Cooper moved forward to get his input on Mike. "What you say will be safe with us. No one will know you spilled the beans. We just want to find out who did this to Jonathan so this won't happen again. We know you had some strong ties with the guy. We want to know anything you've got. The smallest things can be a huge help."

Mike looked to the ground and nodded slowly. "We don't know..."

Williams crossed his arms. "What do you mean you don't know?"

"I mean we don't know," Mike shrugged. "It just happened without warning. Jonathan was big, but still small enough that they could find him."

Myles raised an eyebrow. "Who's 'they?'"

Mike shrugged. "I don't know... maybe another

gang; the one who done him in. Look, I can't be seen out in the open talking to y'all. I'd get murdered myself for running my mouth."

Cooper reassuring Mike. "All we need is a name."

"We don't know," Mike whimpered. "If anything, it has to be *The Sin*."

Williams put his hands on his hips. "Sounds like a bunch of pre-teens trying to sound cool. What kind of name is The Sin?"

Mike laughed. "Right? Well, it looks like they're not just some pre-teens looking for trouble. One of our guys are dead, and the boss is flipping out over it. I'd say if you don't find out who did it soon, there's gonna be a whole lot more death."

Cooper brought out a notepad. "Could you give us a specific name?"

Mike was silent for a moment as he thought. "Try Stewart Bobby. He'd for sure give you what you're looking for."

Cooper smiled, handing a card to Mike. "Thank you, Mike. If you come up with any other ideas about who could've done this, please don't hesitate to call us. Remember Mike, every little detail matters."

Myles started up his car, letting it idle for a moment. "Ahh, sweet progression. At least we've got a name down."

Cooper smiled cockily. "Not without my help."

Myles made a slight sarcastic smirk as he shook his head. "If you're going to do that every time you do your job, I don't think I'll be able to work with you anymore."

"Come on," Cooper insisted. "That was pretty good for my first try."

"Don't push it," Myles turned to the steering of his car.

Right as Myles was about to pull away from the curb, Williams' voice came from the receiver. "Hey... I think Karter is in some trouble. Heard something about another murder related to our case. It's just a few blocks north from here."

Myles was intrigued. "On my way."

Myles saw a few cop cars in the parking lot near the warehouse. They had already busted down one of the doors and were scanning the inside for anything that could potentially be important for the detectives by marking it with a yellow tab. As he pulled up, he saw what looked like Karter sitting on an old bench near the warehouse. There was a paramedic at the scene to treat Karter since he did have a few scrapes and cuts. It didn't seem apparent to Karter that there was a gash across his leg where the skin caught on to the metal scaffolding as he fell. Karter just stared off into space as a security blanket laid gently over him.

Myles walked over to Karter; Cooper and Williams followed. Myles was surprised to see Karter so spooked; he was shaking and shivering, and his skin was a pasty shade of white. Myles could tell he was going through shock. He decided to sit down next to him, wrapping an arm around him.

"You alright? You don't seem so good." Myles could notice that Karter's breathing was irregular, and his pupils were enlarged.

"I feel like throwing up..." Karter answered with a slight whimper in his voice.

Myles didn't know what Karter experienced, but it was obviously something that could've traumatized him.

"How'd you get your leg cut up?" Myles inquired. "Looks like you may need to get stitches."

"I didn't want to work alone..." Karter steered away from the question. "My director said it was just questioning though, so I didn't need a partner... He wasn't at his house so I went to his work... I saw his car in the parking lot, but all the doors were locked... I knew it was dangerous, and I should've waited for backup in case he had a weapon... I was just in the moment... and boy did that change once I actually saw him..."

Myles knew it was hard to repeat details, but as an investigator, they have to ask questions. "How did you get inside?"

"I fell through the second-floor balcony..." Karter recalled. "It was like entering a whole new world... If I saw anything move, I swear I would've shot it... I've never been so scared of the dark before... I felt like I was 10 years old going through some abandoned warehouse... And the smell... Then... I saw him... His lifeless body was standing straight up like some sick puppet show... He was displayed just like all the other animals in the warehouse... He'd been sitting there longer than Jonathan, and no one knew... He was stitched up and..." Karter stopped before leaning over and dry heaving.

Myles rubbed his back gently, and once finished, pulled Karter into a gentle hug. It was frightening for Myles to see Karter like this. Myles put a hand on Karter's head, pulling him into a closer hug. "It's alright big guy, we'll take it from here. Take a break and clear your mind. You weren't expecting what you saw." Myles could feel how fast Karter's heart was beating. It was like a hard bass drum in his chest.

Williams didn't know what to say. He was in a squat looking at Karter. "You handled the situation well. It takes a lot to do a thing like that."

Cooper was silent as if he didn't know what to say either. He didn't seem to be prepared for a case like this. Seeing a detective like Karter go through something like this could put a new cop through a lot of stress, though Cooper looked like he had the ambition to investigate. "How did you get out if all the doors were locked?" Cooper inquired. "I thought warehouse locks from the inside and out."

Karter looked over to Cooper, who had yet to introduce himself. "I pushed a stuffed bear near the hole I fell out of and just climbed out... Once I was out, I called for help." Karter was released from the hug Myles gave, so he sat back up. "Work smart, not hard," he stated. "I was being stupid; I should've called for help before I did anything. How can I be a cop if I can't handle seeing a dead body like that?"

Myles shook his head. "Doesn't just sound like a dead body to me. Sounds like you saw a body that had been mutilated."

The way Myles described it made Karter dry heave again. Cooper looked like he had enough, starting to walk towards the scene of the crime; not before being stopped by Myles. "You're not going in there," Myles ordered as he stood up.

Cooper seemed a little insulted. "Why not? It's my job."

Myles walked forward, putting a hand on Cooper's shoulder. "Once you see it, you won't be able to sleep for weeks. I'm not about to have a spooked recruit scared out of his job. You're still important; we need you here. People like me and Williams and even Karter have seen things like this all the time."

Cooper looked down, then back at Myles. "How do you guys do it?"

Myles raised an eyebrow. "Do what?"

"How do you guys cope with what you see?"

It took a while for Myles to think of a possible answer. He didn't want to frighten Cooper, but he felt like he should give him the truth. "We're all human; we don't deal with it. After a while, you'll just become desensitized. When you start your first big case and you see stuff like this... it changes you."

Midnight had finally set in; Cooper sat outside waiting for anyone to come out of the building with details of the scene. Karter had been taken to the hospital for stitches, and Sergeant Williams was on the phone with an FBI supervisor, so Cooper was stuck twirling his thumbs. Finally, Myles and Hayden emerged from the building with nothing important at hand – besides Myles – who had a drawing. He looked over to Cooper and gave the sketch to him.

"Alright Cooper, let's see how well your detective skills are. I have the scene sketched down on that paper. The first floor is on the first page, and the second is on the last page." Myles pointed to all the known evidence found at the scene. "There are bullet casings near the back of the building. All of the bullets that go to these casings were found scattered around the room from a distance of 11 feet. The casings also look to be 9mm. A trail of dried blood can be seen leading to a room with a body. There's also a few drops of fresh blood leading to the hole where Karter fell, but we all know who it belongs to of course. There's a mac-10 fifteen meters from where the casings are as well, which is outside of the normal cache. Under a rug in the main office, there's a little storage of many weapons. Inside some of the taxidermy animals are also many varying types of class A drugs. In the room off to southeastern part of the building is a body. The body is unrecognizable but has an ID belonging to Erik Vincent. The victim has a rod coming up into the anus, ripping through the abdominal cavity, giving the victim the illusion of standing straight up."

Cooper cringed to the thought, but Myles and Hayden showed little to no reaction to it. Myles kept listing the details. "Two stab marks on the chest, three in abdominal, all of which have been stitched up. There is another cut going down the median of his torso, in which all of his major organs were removed and replaced with cotton. All missing organs were dumped in front of the body, which is now all in a mushy slime state. Skin is leathery, darkening with color; eyes have been removed and replaced with glass animal eyes. The mandible is missing, but still has the tongue hanging from the hyoid bone which still remains attached. Inside the slimy residue of decomposed organs is a black chess piece: the knight. On the wall nearest to the body, there are words written in dried blood. The words read, 'Those yond sineth shalt meeteth grievance.'"

Cooper thought for a while on the subject before stating his observations. "Well, it is clear that it's related to the last case, right? Karter found a black pawn at the last scene, and now there's a black knight here. The difference between this death and the last is that this murder was a lot more passionate. The suspect clearly wanted to set a tone for whoever found the body. The skin is leathery though, and the organs have already been turned into a slushy. I'd say this body has been there for weeks, if not days. That'd mean that he had been murdered before Jonathan. The message on the wall is questionable though; 'Those yond sineth shalt meeteth grievance?' That doesn't sound like anything that some gang off the streets would say."

Myles glanced at his wristwatch before continuing. "Well, our only lead right now is The Sin. We could try asking around for who could've done this, but I don't think we'll be so lucky as we were today."

Cooper went on and followed Myles as he walked towards his car. "For all we know, it may be The Sin. Then again, Mike could've just lied to us to cover up the full picture."

"Don't be so daft," Hayden added as Myles reached into his glove compartment and pulled out some pills. "He could've just lied so you'd let him off on his merry way."

Myles started to accumulate spit in his mouth as he spoke. "Honestly, he really just sounded like he was clueless as to who was killing their guys." He then swallowed a pill.

Cooper didn't appear to be completely satisfied with their findings. "Well, so far there are two people from the same gang dead. They did happen to know each other though, in fact, they happen to work with each other. It may just be some crazy druggy that got sold out of his sniff."

Hayden shook his head. "This was too organized to be some random addict."

Cooper extended his arms. "Has anyone thought about the reason for the chess pieces? A dealer being the pawn; someone that the gang can live without and easily replace. Still has value and gets the job done, but there's so many of this piece that they're easy to come by."

"Jonathan Martly was important though," Hayden asserted. "He was probably the biggest dealer in the gang."

"Which is exactly why he was more in the line of sight to kill," Myles proclaimed. "The farther a pawn is down the board, the closer it is to becoming something bigger like a queen for example. He'll then become dangerous, and a high threat to the opponent." Myles then paused. "What about Erik? If that's Erik in there, then he'd be the knight. The knight is still in a risky position, but it's more valuable. It's the only other one besides the pawn that can start the game. The knight cuts corners and makes the deal, much like what Erik did."

"What are you trying to say?" Hayden inquired.

"I'm saying what if The Sin is trying to take out the Aesthetics? The role of the game is to take out the king. The only question is what's the next move the opponent will make."

"It's the other sides move now though," Cooper acknowledged. "And we don't know what they are going to do next."

As they spoke amongst themselves, Sergeant Williams walked up to the detectives, cutting into the conversation. "Well, I just got off the phone with a FBI supervisor. They said that since Karter hasn't been working in the force for too long, he may, unfortunately, be fired."

Myles' face turned into concern. "What? Why?"

Williams cleared his throat. "Well, Karter did break into the building without proper reason."

"He didn't mean to though, he fell in!" Cooper interrupted.

Williams started making a stern face. "Cooper, I did everything I could. I'm not your gossip buddy and I know you're new, so I don't want to argue." He then turned to Myles. "I know he's your pal, but this is completely out of my control. His blood is all over the crime scene. Best case scenario: He'll just get a bad record and be let off the case." The three detectives looked at each other, but out of all of them, Myles was the most distraught. There was a silence among them, so Williams decided to end the conversation there. "I'm going to the hospital to break the news. I assume all of you have scanned the scene, and done everything you're supposed to do, so go ahead and gather evidence."

Myles looked down to Cooper. "Better go with him. I'm sure Karter would like the company."

FIVE

STITCHES

Karter was still in his brown button-up shirt; he wore the same clothes from earlier, though his pants had been ripped near the inside of his right calf, showing a stitched up scar on his leg, which went up to his knee. It was already past midnight, so Cooper started to develop dark shades under his eyes. Williams had already confronted Karter about what could happen to him so Cooper could comfort him now that the Sergeant was out of the room. From the look on Karter's face, he was not happy about it.

"Hey, Karter," Cooper solemnly greeted. "How's your leg?"

"I'll live. I'm more concerned about what'll happen to me and my job."

Cooper pulled a chair next to Karter and sat down. "You never know, they may just let you off on a warning."

"Yeah, and the case," Karter added.

"Don't let it get to you. There was nothing you could've done. It was an honest accident."

"I'll try not to think about it, but no promises." Karter paused before going on. "I was never able to get your name before. I was meaning to ask, but I'm sure I was not myself earlier."

"The name's Cooper. I'm Myles' assistant."

"A fresh new recruit aye? How's the detective work for ya?"

Cooper sounded a bit unsure. "It's been alright."

"You don't sound so confident about that."

"It's wonderful; it's everything I dreamed of. It's just... I don't feel like I fit in with the other officers at the academy. Everyone looks down at you as the 'new guy.'"

Karter sat straight up, giving his attention to Cooper. "What makes you say that?"

"Well... Anderson never really seemed confident in picking me to be on his force."

"Anderson? Isn't he the director of that police department? That's typical director characteristics. You can't let him get you down."

"It's not just him though." Cooper looked down. "What about Sergeant Williams? If I ever come across his office, he makes me get him a cup of joe or something. He treats me like the new kid, or as an intern."

"Just that?" Karter's eyebrows raised. "Come on, that's a sign that he's comfortable with you. Take that as a good chance to get to know him and become friends with him. If it's the fact he's bossing you around, just say no; easy as that. Come on, what's really getting you down?"

Cooper shifted in his chair before continuing. "I don't feel like Myles likes me. Neither does Hayden. Myles always has that face of irritation, and I don't know what to say to liven the mood. He's really serious about his work, and I can tell. I just feel like it's demeaning when he talks to Hayden differently than me."

"Ahhh, that's just good ol Myles for ya. I've known him for a while now, and he was like that for me too. Don't take it personally; he may seem like some bad-tempered cop who hates his job, but he has his moments." Karter paused. "As for Hayden... I'm not sure I ever warmed up to him. He just doesn't like meeting new people. Hayden knew Myles a little longer than I have, and he's never really been open. Maybe that's just something you could figure out."

"How did you and Myles first meet?" Cooper inquired.

"Heh, I honestly can't remember. We've worked on a lot of cases together." Karter paused trying to remember his first encounter with the tall officer. "I think the first time we met was in some sort of shootout. I was on a case where some guy killed his wife and her lover. He lived in Washington originally but moved down here in Palm City to see his family. I was working with all of California's regions just to figure out where the guy was. That's when I met Myles; he was a lot less experienced though, and still had a buzz cut from basic training. He probably wasn't as far into the force as you are now, but then again, neither was I at the time. Eventually, we found the guy staying at an apartment, but he got some kind of hint that we were coming, so there was a shootout. Hayden, Williams, and even Anderson were there."

"Anderson? But isn't he a director?"

"He sure is," Karter smiled. "But at the time, he was still an officer. Quite an experienced officer, but still an officer nonetheless. It wasn't until recently that

Anderson became director, lucky guy. By that time, I'm sure Sergeant Williams wasn't even a Sergeant yet. Actually, I think Anderson worked right next door to Myles. I still don't think it's been taken yet."

"Nah, not yet." Cooper shook his head. "There's an empty office to the right of Myles' office; to the left is Hayden's office, and to the right of the empty office is Williams."

"Still on the fourth floor?" Karter inquired.

"Yup, still on the fourth floor."

"Really? After all these years, they still work there? They've stayed there ever since I met them. I guess they're just really good neighbors."

Cooper let out a sigh. "They seem like such a great team. They've been like that since they met, and I'm just some newbie."

"Don't think that way. They were all someone's apprentice at some point. Myles and Hayden were probably apprentices of Williams, and Anderson was still taking orders from whoever had more authority than him. He still does too; it's just that that person is now an official for a couple departments now. Long before Hayden and Myles came around, Williams was probably called an apprentice by Anderson. Anderson had friends that he worked for that Williams wanted to fit in with, and the director that Anderson took orders from was simply a Sergeant once. Years from now, you'll look at everything you went through and know that it all just takes time to fit in. Someday you'll have a recruit following you around, and you'll remember the times you were so naive. By that time, someone like Myles or Hayden could be the director; crazy to think of, right?"

Cooper seemed a little more reassured. "Thanks

Autumn. I'm glad I could be able to vent out to someone about—"

"What did you call me?" Karter interrupted.

"Autumn? I heard Myles refer to you as Autumn before, and didn't know if that was your real name or not."

Karter groaned. "It's my middle name and the guys call me that because I'm ginger."

"Heh, honest mistake. Didn't mean to make fun of ya or anything."

Karter cracked a smile. "Stick with Karter and you'll be fine."

There was a moment of silence before Cooper spoke. He rubbed the back of his head. "I came here to make sure you were alright, but I guess the roles flipped."

Karter lifted his hand, swatting away at the air. "Don't worry about it. I'm an officer. I like to help people."

"What is it like to be in the FBI?" Cooper inquired.

"It's quite a serious job; it can get scary at times though. The rules used to be 'if the FBI were on a case, they'd basically trump everyone else.' Now that there are zones, the FBI has lost that reputation. Zones are very important to our modern society, so they go hand and hand with the FBI. It's honestly like two competitors though. I do have my times where I work with the regional departments, but other times I'm completely alone. I have my own job to prioritize, and it's only luck when I run into a crime that they're also occupying."

Cooper – like anyone else – showed interest in the stories Karter had to tell. "What would you say is the scariest case you've worked on?"

Karter put a finger on his chin as he thought for a

moment. "If I had to be honest, it'd be this case we're on now. It's really disturbing." There was another pause before Karter continued. "And I hate mannequins... Fake animals count too." Karter shivered aggressively to the thought of what happened earlier. "It's just really unnerving to me. If not the one we're on now, I'd have to say the case I was on last year. Some folks down in southern California were disturbed by some sort of clown stalking them. There were other sightings from their neighbors and surrounding towns too. It was just some real creepy business, but nothing really serious. The reason I was called down there was for the kidnapping of a little girl that lived at one of the remote homes. Imagine how terrifying it'd be to be kidnapped on some huge plot of land by some psycho clown? What's even scarier is having a nine-year-old child go missing."

Cooper had a look of remorse for the little girl. "What happened to her..?"

"Well, after a week or two of investigating, we found where the suspect lived. He lived in an old abandoned house off the land which had been in a fire a few years back. There was an old cellar where the girl was kept. The poor girl was malnourished. Thankfully, she kept her innocence, and only had a few minor cuts and bruises."

"And the clown was caught?"

"Yeah, he came back to the abandoned house shortly after and was sentenced a long time. It was also my most successful case yet. It was like a happy ending; everything worked out in the end. I'm guessing some old man got lonely and kidnapped himself a girl. Still stands as a really creepy case."

"Yeah... I couldn't imagine how much stress you were going through."

"Kidnappings aren't exactly what I do," Karter claimed. "I'm usually a detective that solves murders, but I'm open to anything really. I'm still really new to the force, and my director wants to see what I'm capable of doing." Karter's face then turned into a sad expression.

"What's wrong?" Cooper inquired.

"I just hope this one slip up isn't the end of my career."

"From the sound of all the success you've had, I don't think they could afford to lose you."

Karter sighed. "It's not like they have any choice though. What I did was against the law, and they have to hold me accountable for it."

Cooper patted Karter's back. "Don't think too much about it mate; things will always get better."

SIX

SLEEP

Myles looked at his wristwatch, noticing how late it was; he could practically feel himself drifting to sleep. By this time, the detective's job was finished, and all that was left was for a full clean up of the crime scene. Sergeant Williams had just made it back from the hospital.

Myles looked around. "Where's Cooper?"

"He's with Karter. They were having a conversation when I walked in, so I didn't want to be rude. It might do the new guy a little good to talk to Karter."

"They've got no ride though," Myles rubbed his eyes.

"I'll make sure to pick them up from the hospital eventually." Williams put his hand on Myles' shoulder. "You look tired; why don't you go home and get some sleep?"

Myles tried holding back a yawn. "A little coffee is all I'll need."

Williams put his hands on his hips. "I know you haven't gotten a decent amount of sleep in a while.

Go home and get some rest. You've done your job for the day."

"What about all the evidence?" Myles questioned. "I'll need to go through it as soon as possible."

"I'll make sure to put it in your lab tonight. Really Myles, go home."

Myles swatted his hand in front of his face. "Okay, okay. Let me just get my stuff."

It was a calm fall morning; Myles had no intention of sleeping tonight though. He wanted to get all the evidence processed before he went in to question the gang Mike was talking about. He picked up his police tape inside the building, noticing Hayden hunched down, looking at the pile of liquefied organs on the ground.

"Hey, I'm gonna go home and get some sleep," Myles yawned. "You gonna be here all night?"

Hayden seemed a bit tired himself. His voice was deep and worn out. "Yea. I'll see you in the morning."

"I think we have a lead," Myles stated.

"Huh?" Hayden looked back.

"Williams and I questioned a guy named Mike. He's part of the gang Aesthetics. He said it may be a rivaling gang called 'The Sin.' I'll tell you more about it tomorrow, but I think we should all head over to their side of the neighborhood and ask around."

"Sound good to me," Hayden responded. "Stay safe, bud."Hayden looked back at Myles.

The statement caught Myles off guard. "You too," he replied as he went for the door.

The ride home was relaxing and silent; Myles caught himself dosing off a couple of times, entranced by the flashing lights of the street lamps passing overhead. The city buildings that touched the sky were built in odd shapes and sizes. It almost seemed like little glass needles were stuck between the ground and the clouds. These tall building designs looked artistic in nature rather than a structurally safe monument; buildings gave the impression to defy the laws of physics and to take a design to a whole new level. High landings were created from building to building like some interconnected web. These long and narrow bridges between skyscrapers were like highways of the working class. In relation to this, the fear of heights couldn't have been an attribute of the modern business employee.

Myles noticed electronic billboards scattered ahead from the highway, all of which seemed to be focused around one point. One billboard in particular read "We could've saved it," with a picture of Earth turning gray and dried up. Another billboard was a little more enthusiastic about the matter. The letters "We have a plan," were in bold; all above the heads of the brave men and women that landed on Mars. Other billboards seemed to be for charity to help cities across the world that didn't have clean drinking water due to pollution.

By this year, all petrol vehicles had stopped being produced for civilian purposes. Even though humanity found new ways of reaching this valuable liquid, Earth's health was plummeting fast. This is what led to regulations on gasoline fed cars, so much so, that it was almost impossible to create an efficient petrol vehicle. This lead to a large increase in electric cars being produced.

Aluminum cars also became a reoccurring characteristic of this time period. Myles' car, however, was a very old design. In 2025, a car producing company created a project on old looking cars and produced a special model. This model most resembled the 1971 Plymouth Barracuda, fitted with a supercharged V8, all being manual stick shift. Originally, it was sold only for a limited amount of time; Myles didn't want it any other way, so he made sure to reach the certain requirements that were needed to make it a police cruiser. By this time, cars started to lose MPH over fuel-efficient standards, which was later outdone by electric cars. This 66-year-old car had its mileage done for, and Myles was just about finished with it; though he grew fond of it. By now he was certain that every part of the vehicle had been replaced, and gasoline was extremely hard to find at this age. Nevertheless, he decided to keep this classic model.

As Myles pulled into the parking lot, he could feel something go wrong in his car. He was sure that he'd have to fix it eventually but was too tired to do it at the moment. He made sure to grab his lab coat from the back seat to protect him from the freezing breeze; his black sweater could only keep him warm for so long. He fumbled a bit at his front door, trying to find the key to his apartment room; his hands were just itching to grab a cigarette from his jacket. The heater turned on as he entered his sketchy, run-down home. He could hear shouting through his thin walls; fighting was a commonplace in his apartment complex. Nevertheless, Myles was determined to get a good night's rest. After finishing a cigarette or two, Myles crept into something comfy and rolled into bed.

The transition from real to dream state was almost instant; by the blink of an eyelid, Myles felt himself drift into a deep sleep. At first, he felt himself in some slur of darkness but soon started drifting through space like a shooting star. The vast, immense galaxy was right at his fingertips; nothing to stop him, and only the universe as his bounds. He slowly recoiled himself into a capsule; the weightless feeling made his stomach stimulate. Out the window was a massive structure of rusty red formations. He could only identify it as a distant planet in our solar system: Mars. As his mind wandered, he felt gravity slowly regain itself upon Myles, slowly descending through the clouds of this planet.

As he fell through the atmosphere, a bloom of colors started to appear, and his capsule started to dissolve. A bluish liquid started to surround Myles, giving the illusion of water. The bright bloom of bluish colors started to fade darker and darker as he fell deeper and deeper into the planet until he was floating in nothing but pitch darkness. Myles looked out into the distance, spotting an array of colors. Red, orange, yellow, green, blue, indigo, violet; the fluttering colors of jellyfish surrounded Myles, speaking to him in whispers. He tried speaking but choked on the thin air around him.

The colors started to fade further, falling within the deep blue darkness. As the colors faded, the background washed away, making shapes and objects. Myles started to regain consciousness, finding himself behind the wheel of his vehicle. He was at a street light which had just turned red. He looked at his clock, reading that it wasn't even a quarter past 3. His phone buzzed, which showed an unrecognized caller ID; the message sent that spread across the screen made Myles' eyes water.

"Why here… I can't let it happen again…"

The light turned green, so Myles started to accelerate forward. He looked to his left, seeing lights in the distance coming towards him at an alarming rate. It seemed to all happen so quickly; the front of a vehicle intersected Myles' car, ripping into the cab of the vehicle. The sound was defining, ripping the metal and steel until nothing was left but a mess of scrap. Myles was ejected a few feet from the wrecked car; body bent back and lifeless. The car was going so fast that Myles' car was completely wrapped around it; after which was only deafening silence.

"Um... would you like more water?"

Myles jolted awake, looking around him. He seemed to be at some 24-hour restaurant. It was still dark outside, and beside him was a girl taking his order. He had some fries in front of him that had turned cold and soggy. Myles looked up to see a waitress checking up on him.

"Oh... no, sorry." Myles smiled as he looked up to her.

The girl walked away, but Myles seemed distraught. He looked down at his hands, counting his fingers after taking in a deep breath of air.

"One... Two... Three... Four..."

He seemed more and more nervous as he tried finding his fifth finger. His heart started to beat faster and faster as he tried finding his missing finger. Then, just as he found his fifth finger, a massive crash was heard from outside, startling Myles. Looking outside, he observed a massive wreck at an intersection. His first instinct was to get up and investigate. Everyone else at the restaurant looked outside, astonished by what they had just witnessed.

Myles ran as fast as he could towards the mangled

mess of steel scattered about the intersection; a car seemed to have T-boned another. Myles raced to the first car, seeing a man behind the wheel; blood poured from his face as he sat there in silence.

"Excuse me..? Can you hear me?" Myles inquired.

The man looked over to Myles with a look of dread. "Have you come to get your revenge..?"

Myles seemed unsure. "What do you mean..?"

The man started to look offended. "Don't act like you don't know what just happened... I killed you..."

Myles' eyes started to water as he looked over to the mangled mess beside him. "Who was in the car..?"

"It doesn't matter anymore..." The man put his head on the bent steering wheel. "It's been pulverized... I got a glimpse of someone, but... he looked just like you."

Myles looked at the mangled mess again. "There's just never enough time..."

The man grabbed the collar of Myles' shirt, pulling him in close. "Don't take it personal, kid."

A loud buzzer went off, making Myles jolt awake. He sat straight up in his bed, sweating bullets. The sun was just starting to bloom over the horizon, peaking into Myles' bedroom. Everything turned deathly silent, except for his phone alarm which he then turned off.

SEVEN

TEETH

"Intel says they should be at either of these houses. We gotta hurry though," Hayden spoke through the radio.

Myles sat straight up in his car seat, eyeballing people as he entered a neighborhood. A few days before, an officer found out exactly where Stewart Bobby lingered around. Because of this, the detectives were able to identify other group members and hideouts. In the passenger seat was, of course, his partner Cooper, who was checking the street addresses. Hayden and Williams drove in a separate vehicle though; they were in groups of two in case of being outnumbered. There was some reconnaissance, which stated that members of the gang "Sin" were supposedly seen at two locations. It was early in the morning, so there wasn't much commotion outside. Myles held a cigarette between his index and middle finger, taking a puff every so often.

"684..." Cooper repeated as he looked at the house numbers. "It's around here somewhere, I'm sure of it."

Myles looked ahead, noticing a run-down house to

his right. There were three people on the porch, all in chairs. "Is that it right there?"

After a moment of silence, Cooper confirmed it with a nod. "They don't look friendly."

Myles took one last puff before smooshing the cigarette down into a pot he had in the backseat. "They never are. Just be on high alert. This is the only lead we have, so we could possibly be running into a murderer."

Myles and Cooper stepped out of their car, walking at a steady pace towards the house. The people on the porch started to stand up, eyeballing the officers. Myles wore a black zip-up hoodie to give him a less intimidating look. Underneath the jacket was a bulletproof vest, which chafed into his arms. His badge was hanging from a necklace, showing his department. Cooper, on the other hand, went with a more aggressive look, revealing his body armor.

"Excuse me?" one of the men on the porch spoke as he walked down to the officers. He was quite a tall and robust man. "What's going on here?"

Myles decided to speak in a monotone voice, remaining calm and collected. "We're part of the PCPD. There's been a murder a few blocks from here. Two members of the gang, Aesthetics, were found, and they believe it may be because of the gang 'Sin.'"

The man seemed irritated by this response. "So you're just gonna come in here and accuse us of something we never even done?"

Myles saw a bit of tension in the subject. "Sir, we aren't going to accuse you of anything, we're just trying to get a little bit of insight. May we search your home and car?"

"Say again?" The man started to clench his fists.

"May we search your belongings?" Myles repeated. "It would help us out tremendously."

"I must be hearing the wrong thing." The man yelled, starting to get the attention of the other men. "I thought I heard you ask if you could search my house!" The other men on the porch started to come down to see what was going on.

"You heard correct," Cooper intervened. "We can't search your things without your consent, but if you aren't comfortable with it, then we don't have to search anything. Instead, we could just talk."

The man still seemed reluctant. "How is searching my belongings going to help you? What if the Aesthetics are just lying to get us in jail? Did you ever think about that?"

The man was right, but it wasn't like their innocence was on the line. Myles went on. "If you have nothing to do with this murder, you're perfectly safe. We already know that the gang you're in comes in and out of your house. If we find anything illegal, there's no telling who it belongs to. You won't get charged for that." Cooper looked up to Myles, making a strange face.

The man took a step towards Myles, trying to intimidate the officer. "Get off my property."

The sudden step forward made Myles and Cooper both reach for their belts to grab some utility. "Step away," Myles spoke calmly as he put a hand on his taser.

The man seemed more irritated than before, taking another step toward the officer. "I ain't gonna tell you again. Leave my property."

Hayden and Williams were at the other end of the neighborhood, looking for another home with

Sin members inside. The sun had been beating down through the right-side window, giving Williams quite a burn. Balls of sweat rolled down his darkened skin.

"There," Hayden pointed.

As they left their vehicles, they immediately noticed the snarling dog, chained to the fence. The door opened up, showing a young man with a hat and a white t-shirt, trying to find the source of all the commotion.

"Evening sir." Sergeant Williams spoke in a friendly tone. "Why don't you step out here for me?"

The man, obviously confused, stepped down cautiously. "What's this for?"

"Mind if we pat you down?" Hayden asked the man.

Williams reached up and silenced his partner. "I've got this." He then turned to the fedora-sporting man. "Have you heard the name Jonathan Martly and/or Erik Vincent anywhere?"

The man shook his head once again. "No o'sifer. Never in my life." The man didn't seem stocky at all; his arms were like noodles. Williams was starting to think they had the wrong house.

Eventually, Hayden started to get annoyed by the dog barking. "Hey, could you put a cork in that thing?"

The man turned around and clapped his hands loudly, bringing the dog's attention to him. "Come on girl, it's alright. They ain't gonna hurt you."

"Do you happen to know anyone that has more information about Jonathan and Erik?" Williams asked the man.

"Probably the source of it all," the man wiped his nose. "Talk to Andrew Sutton. He's part the Aesthetics too, and he's one of the higher ups, so he'd know more than me."

Williams and Hayden smiled to each other. "I don't recall mentioning The Aesthetics," Hayden noted.

"I thought that was what we were referring to," the man nervously stuttered.

"I thought you'd never heard those names in your life," Williams recalled.

"Come on," the man held his hands up. "I was exaggerating. I meant that I don't know a lot about them."

Hayden stepped forward with a notepad. "Well? What do you know?"

The man sighed. "Just that they ran into a bit of trouble, and some of their guys died. Some shootout or something."

Even though Hayden and Williams seemed sure that that's not what happened, they wanted to see what exactly was going around. "What kind of trouble? Who killed who?"

The man looked like some kid trying to look calm but came off as nervous. "I heard about some sort of money handling deal that went wrong, and now they got some enemies."

"Did they happen to be part of your gang?" Williams inquired.

"Nah, Nah," The man laughed. "We don't just go lookin' around for trouble. We don't talk to The Aesthetics."

Myles put a hand out, gently pushing the bulky man back. "I asked you to step back sir."

The man still resisted, stepping up to Myles. "You touch me again, you're losing your arms!"

Cooper started to intervene, extending his hand

between Myles and the man. "Relax, we aren't here to fight."

"I got this," Myles reassured Cooper, starting to regret his carelessness actions. "Could you calm down sir?"

"I ain't calming down until you're gone!" The man took another large step towards Myles.

Myles pushed the man back again, but this time more forcefully. "Relax!" Myles spoke more aggressively, attempting to appear formidable. He wrapped his hand around his taser, pulling it out, but without a second thought, the stocky man yanked Myles' badge down and connected with a vigorous, powerful uppercut to Myles' jaw. The hit left Myles disoriented on the ground.

Cooper tried reaching for his sidearm, but the man's accomplices lunged towards the officer, tackling him to the ground. Before Myles could react, the built man sat on his stomach, holding Myles' throat down, trying to strangle him. Myles tightly gripped the wrists of the man, kicking to no avail; blood started to flow to the back of his throat. He couldn't see what they were doing to Cooper; all he could see was the face of a man trying to kill him. His taser was just beside him, so he reached for it as he started to turn blue and dizzy. Without hesitation, Myles pulled the trigger right into the abdominal region of the stocky man. With a scream and howl, the man stiffened up, falling to the floor.

Myles could feel the blood flow back into his head as the grip of the stocky man was released. As he stood up, he could see Cooper being beat to a pulp. One man held him down as the other pounded him.

"Hooper!" Myles yelled out as he pulled out his Glock, pointing it to the men. "Pu yur han up!" Myles shouted furiously, finding it difficult to speak.

The men holding Cooper down put their hands up, seeing their friend on the ground moaning as he doubled over in pain. Myles spat out a chunk of bloody teeth as he stared the men down.

He then felt a hand rest on his shoulder. At first, he was startled and expecting to fight but was relieved to see it was Hayden. "Whoa... It's just me, calm down," Hayden reassured Myles.

Williams stepped forward, shouting at the men with his gun drawn. "Get on the ground now!"

The tossing and turning left Myles breathless. He walked over to the stocky gentleman, wrapping his arms behind his back to handcuff him. It took a lot longer than expected to get him in cuffs because his shoulders were too broad; it took two handcuffs to reach each arm. By the time Myles got the beefy man in handcuffs, Hayden and Williams had already got his accomplices bound.

"Hooper? You ohay?" Myles asked quite concerned for his partner.

His face was red and swollen, but it didn't seem like that was the worst of it. He was doubled over, holding his stomach.

Hayden looked to Myles, seeing the blood dripping from his chin. "What the hell happened to you!"

"I bih my houne." Myles tried to speak, but couldn't over the fact that he was bleeding profusely, and his teeth were shattered.

Hayden seemed a lot more concerned than he should've as he crouched down to Cooper. As Hayden checked on their new officer, the dread of the situation started to become a reality. "We're gonna have to call an ambulance... I don't think Cooper is breathing..."

EIGHT

COMA

Myles felt as though he couldn't breathe. His tongue had started swelling up, and the gauze in his mouth didn't help. When he received the forceful uppercut, it shattered his teeth, but in the process bit a chunk of his tongue. Most of the day had gone by, and the doctor had just finished putting his teeth back together. There were a few pieces that were missing since he wasn't able to find the rest, but for the most part, it was all put back into place. As for the missing teeth, the doctor simply filled it temporarily until he could receive better help.

After he was finished talking to the doctor about what's to happen of his teeth, he asked if he could see his partner Cooper.

As he entered his room, he could recognize four people in the room as his fellow officers. Williams, Hayden, and Karter all sat next to each other, and Cooper, of course, was in a bed, resting. A nurse watched as Myles walked in.

"Good news; he's breathing on his own," the nurse

smiled. "You guys really are lucky. I heard you two got into a tussle with some troublemakers."

Myles didn't say anything. It wasn't that he didn't want to talk, but because it hurt to talk; his jaw was unbearably sore.

"Ahem…" the nurse kept talking, worried that she was being too insensitive. "He'll be alright. He's just getting some rest. He's lucky he didn't go into a coma. He's had quite a bit of trauma to the head." After some silence, the nurse decided it was best for her to leave them be. "I'll let you guys do your thing. If you need me, don't be afraid to come down the hall. Watch over him to make sure he's still okay."

As the nurse left, Myles could see how bad the thugs got Cooper; his face was blue and purple. Myles couldn't help but feel responsible for what happened to his partner. He looked over to the three officers who were patiently waiting for a response from Cooper. Sergeant Williams stood up and walked over to the door, waving Myles to go out the hall with him.

"He was awake for a moment before you got here," Williams spoke softly. "He told me about what had happened, and started to go off on himself; telling me that his brothers were right, and how much of a mess up he was."

Myles tried speaking, but the gauze in his mouth mixed with his swollen tongue and sore jaw made it a slobbery, mumbling mess. "We were outnumbered."

"He could've died, Myles." There was some silence before Williams continued. "You can't just roll up to people's houses and tell them you're going to search them without a real good reason."

Myles wiped the slobber that came from his mouth. "We had a witness claim that they were causing it."

"That witness was unsure, and you know that," Williams countered.

"There's no other lead we have," Myles whined. "There is no evidence! What is there to work with when you can't find anything!"

"The plan was to gather information," Williams reminded Myles. "Hayden and I didn't have a violent confrontation, and we learned that The Sin had no idea what was going on. After searching the houses and cars of those three men you encountered, there was nothing to be found. No murder weapon, no single trace of evidence supporting that they are involved."

"I didn't search them though. I was hoping that I could search them with their permission. I was really calm with them too. I was patient," Myles slurred.

"That's not what I heard from Cooper. He said you weren't in the best mood with them."

"I can't help it! I look intimidating, I know, and they may have been rubbed the wrong way!"

"You don't look intimidating now," Williams declared. "You look stupid."

The look on Myles' face went down as he took the insult.

"Myles, you're part of the PCPD," Williams crossed his arms. "You're smarter than this. You're supposed to be better with people and defuse the situation. You're supposed to know ques when a person will take the initiative and become hostile. You're expected to know how to handle a dilemma like this without this outcome."

"It got to a point where he just wasn't reasonable," Myles stated.

"You took too many risks, and it almost got you and Cooper killed. What are you trying to do? Scare the kid out of his job?"

Myles started to tense up. "Look, I was hoping to find something, but I was wrong. It was stupid for me to go down that route. Right now there's a person or group that are roaming around out there free after mutilating two people. If we don't start taking risks, they may keep killing."

"There's a difference between putting yourself in danger, and actually cracking down on someone, Myles! You weren't prepared to go up against those guys, and Cooper certainly wasn't either."

Myles shrugged. "They didn't seem like they'd take it *that* far though..."

Williams rubbed his face. "You trust people way too easily Myles. There's a reason why we handcuff criminals. There's a reason we don't just put criminals in our passenger seat. You can't just trust someone you don't know. You have to visualize the worst scenario so you don't get yourself killed."

Myles paused before speaking. "You may see them as criminals, but that's not what I see. Some of them can't help it. Some of them just have it hard, and can only live off of that lifestyle. It may be against the law, but how far will you go to make sure your family is fed? So maybe they were a little on the edge. Everyone gets to be like that after what they've been through. Who am I to take someone else's life over my own?"

Williams was taken back. "You have a right to defend yourself though. It's a basic human need to stay alive." Williams paused before continuing. "I'm glad no one died, but it got way too close. I just don't want good cops like you and Cooper to die. We need more of you on the streets. You put other lives before your own, and even when they're strangling you to death, you still see them as a person. Why would you ever think in such a broad way?"

Myles paused, trying to think of the answer. "I guess I just trust people too easily."

Williams' face turned serious. "Stop thinking that way then. I don't want to end up at your funeral any time soon. Don't drag Cooper into your stunts either." Williams then turned around and headed inside to sit down. Myles waited outside thinking about what he could've done differently that would've changed what had happened to Cooper. Eventually, he was greeted by Hayden as he came out to check up on him.

"How're the chompers?" Hayden inquired.

"Sucks... I won't be able to smoke for a while. It's gonna be hard." Myles then paused. "I've been getting those nightmares again... The ones where I get into a wreck."

Hayden patted his back gently. "Still can't get that off your mind? Don't worry, I know the feeling. You just gotta tough it out. They'll go away eventually."

"Yeah, but they keep coming back." Myles rubbed his face. "I can't shake them, and I certainly can't change their outcome."

Hayden sighed. "Maybe it's something you just need to accept. You need a find a way to face your fears and regrets so you can get rid of it for good."

"How can I do that though?" Myles inquired.

Hayden smiled. "That's up to you to decide."

"I'll need to do it quick because I can't keep on putting people in danger."

"Hey, the kid's gonna be alright," Hayden reassured. "He'll be back out in no time at all. He just got a little beat up."

"I'm Cooper's supervisor though... I'm supposed to keep him out of trouble. I have to admit, I made some stupid choices."

Hayden put a hand on Myles' shoulder. "There was nothing you could've done. Those guys were a bunch of scum anyways. We've seen far worse than what they'll ever see, yet we're supposed to be the calm and composed ones." Hayden paused. "At least we know more about The Aesthetics. I think we may have got ourselves a new guy to hunt down."

Myles perked up to hearing progress in the investigation. "Oh? Who is it?"

"The guy's name is Andrew Sutton. He's supposedly the one that cooks up all the goodies. He's a big fish, and will certainly provide important information."

"That's great Hayden; I'm glad to see we still haven't dug ourselves into a dead end."

Hayden laughed. "Don't jinx it, man."

The two heard the door open, seeing Karter's head peak out.

"Mind if I come out?" Karter asked.

Hayden seemed a bit less than excited to see Karter. "I might just go sit down. I'll see you two later."

Karter chose to speak once the door was closed after Hayden left. "Poor guy... Cooper's gonna be feeling that for weeks."

"I know..." Myles slumped.

"It'll be alright." Karter patted Myles' shoulder.

"Just give the guy some support. That's all he ever really wanted."

"What do you mean?" Myles inquired. "I support him. I make sure to give him good evaluation reports."

"I mean a pat on the back or some sort of helping hand to make him feel like he's not alone. He'll get to know your personality eventually, but until then, he still needs to be treated like one of you."

"I don't treat him bad. I treat him like an ordinary officer," Myles proclaimed.

"Maybe that's exactly what's wrong." Karter's eyebrow raised. "You gotta know who he is, and what he's like out on the field. You gotta watch over him, but support him when he's making some breakthrough. You out of all people know how hard it is to fit in. Give him a little remorse."

Myles sighed. "I guess you're right. I guess I'll give him a little love here and there."

"That's all it takes," Karter smiled.

There was a slight pause in the conversation before it carried on. Myles looked down to Karter's leg, which had been wrapped. "How's your leg?" Myles asked.

"It hurts of course, but I'll live. I'd prefer not to mention it; the more I think about it, the more it hurts." Karter paused. "That reminds me – I may not lose my job after all!"

Myles seemed joyed to hear this. "I'm glad! You're probably the best detective here."

"Well, that's the problem though." Karter looked down. "I'm off the case you're on so I may not be seeing you very often. To not raise any suspicion, I can't work on this case anymore."

"At least this isn't your last case, right?" Myles reassured. "You still have a great career ahead of you."

Karter sighed. "Yeah, but I was kinda excited to work with the group again. It's always easier as a group. It's also rare when I actually get to see you nowadays."

"There will definitely be a next time though, just remember that. Until then, we'll just be drifting entities floating through the sky, hoping to collide eventually," Myles joked.

NINE

SUSPECT

Hayden was in his office, quietly working on paperwork that he hadn't done the day before – due to the incident – when he heard a knock at the door. Myles appeared, looking as stressed as ever. His whole jaw was now swollen, which made it difficult for him to talk; making his voice sound muffled from the gauze stuffed to the sides of his cheeks to wipe up the fluids. This time was different though. Myles seemed more eager to share what he found.

"I found a suspect," Myles blurted out.

Hayden seemed surprised. "What! Who? What did you find?"

"I was in the lab going through the hair sample we saw in the hallway, and it doesn't hook up to Erik. It actually belongs to a 29-year-old man named Owen Reid. Here's the best part: this man lives 15 miles outside the main city."

Hayden got up from his chair. "Christ Myles, how do we know if the man isn't just some druggy who visited beforehand?"

"He may just have some information we need. That's only if he isn't the killer himself." Myles smirked. "If it is him, he might've taken off a hat, which could've dropped hair or something; I don't know. At least it's someone who knew Erik. You coming with me to crack down on the guy?"

Hayden shook his head. "I really have to catch up with work here. I already missed a day because of everything that happened yesterday."

"Right... Where's Williams?" Myles inquired.

"On the way to the hospital to check up on Cooper," Hayden stated.

Myles' look of confidence went down. "I need someone to have my back when I'm heading down there. There won't be back up for miles. It's outside the boundary of the zone."

"Maybe you should hold back for just today." Hayden sat back down. "Our suspect isn't going anywhere, and he's not tipped off that you're on his tail."

"Don't you think we should snatch him now though so he doesn't take out anyone else?"

"If you're so eager to head down there, why not go get a few officers downstairs to go with you?" Hayden suggested.

Myles sighed. "Well, that's what it's looking like I'm going to have to do."

"How about this: if the guy down in the middle of nowhere isn't who we're looking for, I'll go with you down to look for Andrew Sutton. Deal?"

"I guess so. I'll see you later then." Myles waved goodbye, heading for the door behind him. Before he could shut the door, he heard his name get called out by Hayden. He peeked his head back in.

"Be careful. Don't get into another tussle."

The drive out of the city was dreadful. The traffic was slow, but once off the main highways, it wasn't so bad. Palm City had sections to it; the middle happened to be where the wealthiest people lived. This was also home to a lot of businesses and upper-class workers. Skyscrapers would touch the clouds, and cars would pollute the streets. Around the middle of the city were higher classmen, but not as rich as the center. Buildings were still quite common, but not what one would expect to see towards the middle; a place where PCPD could be seen. This section of the city was actually quite large, but once departed, one would be greeted by a more crude scenery. Coarse, as it may seem, here would be where the lower class workers lived. Some parts of the unrefined section were quite nice, but other parts were home to groups like The Sin and The Aesthetics. Once through the lower class section, one would find themselves going farther down the economic range until they've completely exited the main city; this is normally where the zone would end. There wasn't a lot of citizens discovered out here, normally because all the work is towards the city; nevertheless, it was actually quite a beautiful place. Large plots of land – rich with natural life – were found for the most part; things not prominent in the city would otherwise be discovered here.

In the passenger seat beside Myles was an officer that had been working in the force for three years. She had her hair in a tight pony-tail, which came down to the back or her neck. Behind Myles was another police cruiser with two officers that had been in the force a lot longer. Owen Reid lived on a plot of land that had been passed down to him through the family. His occupation was a mechanic, but it may not be the only thing he does. As the night approached, the horizon radiated with a sublime orange gleam. Myles looked at the clock on his dashboard before speaking to the officer next to him.

"Could you give me the pillbox in the glove compartment?" His mouth was still swollen, and the gauze in his mouth stopped him from ingesting spit, so he decided to spit it out into a cup.

As soon as the officer gave it to him, he popped two into his mouth, swallowing it down with whatever fluids he still had in his mouth. He decided to change out the gauze in his mouth because the previous one seemed to had done its job with soaking blood. The officer beside Myles started to switch the radio on, possibly to break the dead silence in the car.

An announcer spoke on about something they were commercializing. "That's right! Dr. Lindros is someone I trust more than anyone. I'd say that she's one of the greatest minds of the century in terms of biology and genetics."

A female voice came from the radio. "Of course. We have the best engineers working on this one project. We'll be able to change your DNA structure in a matter of days, to the point that you'll have any trait you want! Just as long as these traits are able to fit within your genome."

The announcer sounded enthusiastic. "That's fantastic news! And I did hear that you had a buy one, get one free offer as well?"

"That's right!" Dr. Lindros went on. "We're offering

a tremendous deal! Just be sure to stop by the office soon before time runs out!"

The announcer laughed. "You heard the doctor!"

Myles turned towards the radio and switched it off. He couldn't stand commercials when on duty; besides the fact that they were close to their target. Myles pulled up alongside a dirt road leading to the farm. The police officers got out of their cars, following Myles as he went up to the main house. There seemed to be other structures on the land, but the tall white house was most convincing of residency.

As Myles advanced towards the house, he noticed the front door was wide open. This made Myles uneasy; he put his hand on his sidearm and made a loud knock before yelling out. "Owen Reid? PCPD!"

The house answered with silence. Myles repeated to knock on the door, followed by yelling out their department. The other officers shared a look of unease, only moving along with Myles. Myles took a quick peek inside the house, finding that all the lights were on.

"Owen Reid, are you home?"

No response. Myles thought about the possibility that Owen was simply out on other parts of his farm, so he decided to check the other structures around the plot of land. He gestured at two of the officers.

"You two stay here. If you see movement, call us over."

With two nods, Myles was off with the other officer to see if Owen was anywhere else. As they checked the sheds, they couldn't find anything or anyone whatsoever.

"If I was Owen, where would I be..?" Myles mumbled to himself. The last place to check of course was an old dilapidated pen, which seemed too rusty to still be in use.

"PCPD! Owen Reid! Are you in here!" Myles yelled, grabbing his flashlight to inspect the tall grass and shadows.

Myles entered the pen cautiously; one hand on the handle of his sidearm, and the other holding a flashlight. The officers were startled by a can falling over, which turned out to be a rat moving through the shelves. Myles spotted a note that was left on an old wooden bench. The other officer looked over to him.

"Whatcha got there?"

"It's a note. I think we just missed him..." Myles spoke coldly.

"What's it say?" the officer inquired.

"Look for yourself." Myles moved over to let the other officer get a glimpse at the single piece of paper with the words "missed me" written across it hastily. "Damnit..." Myles cursed his luck. "Who knows how long he's been gone for. It still looks like he really wanted to get out of here fast. Let's get some patrol around here to see if we can catch anything. I'll go check with the neighbors."

The other officer nodded.

Myles banged loudly on the door four times to get the attention of the neighbor. He was greeted by an elderly woman who looked to be in her 80s.

"Excuse me, ma'am," Myles greeted. "I'm part of the PCPD. You mind if I have a talk with you?"

The woman seemed worried. "Of course, come in, come in."

Myles found a seat in the kitchen next to a table.

"Pardon my face; when's the last time you've seen your neighbor?"

The woman calmly sat down across the table to the officer. "I probably haven't seen him for a while now; I can't recall the last time he's been around."

Myles leaned forward. "If you could, it'd be a lot of help to hear some sort of date when you've last seen him."

The woman took a moment to gather her thoughts before she continued. "I think it might've been last Thursday. I usually see him coming down to the road to check his mail. Why? What's happened to him?"

"I don't mean to worry you, but we're on the look for him. Any information would be really helpful. Maybe a place he works at, or some sort of routine he does every day?"

"I'm sorry, I wish I could be more helpful to you," the woman spoke solemnly.

Myles paused. "What would you say his normal behavior has been like? Anything questionable?"

"Not at all," the woman shook her head. "He just seems like a normal Joe. Nice young man."

Myles felt stumped. "I see you have a view of his house from here." He grabbed a card from his jacket, giving it to the woman. "If you see him at all anywhere, please don't hesitate to call this number. It would help us out a lot."

The woman nodded. "I sure will. Thank you, sir."

At a loss again; nothing seemed to come up. It seemed like just whenever they thought they were a step ahead of the suspect, he'd always come out four steps ahead of them. Myles sat on a stool in his lab, looking at the evidence he's gathered from the past crime scenes. He racked himself over the head trying to figure out how exactly they could catch these murderers. He made sure to collect the note from Owen's house as evidence.

"Those yond sineth shalt meeteth grievance..." Myles repeated as he tried to piece together as much as he could.

Myles replayed what Cooper had stated earlier about that phrase. The phrase didn't sound like anything anyone off the street would say. He had a point, and apparently, he was right; the person who wrote the message was from outside of the zone. The question is: why was his DNA found at the scene of Erik Vincent's death? Most importantly, how did he know the cops were coming? Could it be that he left last week, but made it look as though he just left to throw off the police? It was a long shot, but considering how hard it was to find evidence on this guy, it was apparent that the man knew how to get away with murder. Another important question is why? Why did he overgeneralize the murders? Why did he leave behind little chess pieces? Why did he kill these two young men? It seemed almost impossible how their paths would cross... Hayden did say that the Sin member they interrogated thought their deaths were related to some sort of trading ordeal, but of course, he didn't seem like he knew anything; only little rumors.

Could it just be a coincidence that these two murders happened to be in the same gang? Highly unlikely, Myles concluded. Outside of their drug ordeals, these men never spoke to each other; the only history they had with each other was that they went to the same elementary and middle school when they were younger.

Myles rubbed his eyes softly, trying to make sense of what was in front of him. Why so violent? Myles wrote down all of his questions on a sheet of paper to remind himself of the important details. He held the pawn found at Jonathan's murder in front of his face.

"What secrets are you keeping from me?"

TEN

OFFICE

A few days had passed, and Cooper had been recovering. The hospital had finally released him, so Myles decided to pick him up. Cooper still looked banged up from the fight; he had a faint black eye, and still had somewhat of a purple split lip. Myles, on the other hand, didn't need to keep gauze in his mouth anymore, but he still couldn't eat anything without tasting copper. Though his teeth were still healing, he was in a huge withdraw from not smoking for so long. Myles looked to Cooper as they walked up to the main building on campus.

"I feel like I have to say this now before I'm not able to later... I'm really sorry about what happened to you. It was all my fault, and I put your life in danger."

Cooper smiled. "Pfft, don't worry about it; I knew what I was signing up for. Don't think that it was all your fault though; I can't see any way you could've handled it where it wouldn't end up with our lights being punched out."

"Yeah..." Myles still didn't feel completely relieved.

As they walked out of the elevator, Myles grabbed Cooper's shoulder. He covered his eyes and spun him around. Cooper seemed confused.

"What's going on here?" Cooper inquired.

"I've got a little surprise for you. Just close your eyes and don't open them until I tell you to. Got it?"

"You're the boss," Cooper obliged.

As Cooper was led through the hallway, officers started to step out of their offices, trying to keep quiet. Cooper appeared to be completely clueless as to what was going on; he just followed exactly as he was told. Myles led Cooper into a room, signaling other officers to gather around him; that's when Myles removed his hand Cooper's face and asked him to open his eyes. It was just like any room on the fourth floor, except completely empty besides some filing cabinets, a wooden table, and an office chair. Cooper looked around the room, seeing people he knew, as well as officers he hadn't even met before clapping, smiling at him.

"I don't understand... What's this?" Cooper inquired.

"It's your very own office." Sergeant Williams smiled.

Cooper looked closer at what was on the wooden table to see a name imprinted on a stone name tag. It spelled "Officer Alcorn" on it. Cooper's smile extended from ear to ear as he saw his friends greet him. Even Anderson had joined the group, shaking Cooper's hand. Cooper took a quick look outside to see his neighbors. He seemed more than delighted to see it was none other than Myles and Sergeant Williams' rooms.

"Wait..." Cooper paused. "But didn't this used to be Anderson's old office before he became a director?"

Anderson nodded his head. "After a recruit's first

few weeks on the job, they're placed into their own office. I had this office when I was first starting out; had it all the way until I became a director. I was waiting to give the right officer this room, so I decided to give it to you. Welcome to the team."

Cooper looked like he was on the verge of tears; Myles, Hayden, Anderson, Williams, they were all there. It really did make a difference. After all he went through, this was more than a welcoming pat on the back. Williams went over to Cooper, placing a hand on his shoulder.

"To celebrate, we're gonna go out to eat tonight; just the five of us."

"Five?" Anderson questioned.

"You're coming, right?" Williams turned to Anderson. "All on me; I know the best Chinese place in the state. Trust me, it'll be something you won't want to miss."

Anderson shrugged. "I still have a lot to do... But I guess there's nothing wrong with getting a little bit of dinner. Let's just try to get back as soon as we can, alright?"

At the Chinese restaurant, Myles, Cooper, Hayden, Williams, and Anderson all sat outside at a large table meant for large groups. They had already ordered their meals and were currently waiting for them to be ready.

Myles tried staring up a conversation. "So Cooper, how do you like the new office?"

"It's the best! I couldn't have asked for a better room! It's right next to my friends, and it's roomy!"

Myles laughed. "Remember that you're still my partner, and I still have to look over you though," he reminded Cooper.

Williams shifted in his seat. "So, you've got that heavy Australian accent; what part of Australia did you come from?"

Cooper shook his head. "I was actually born in America. I guess I just picked up my accent from my Ma and Pa. I've actually never been to Australia before. Too expensive."

Anderson brought out a pack of cigarettes, bringing one out. He offered one to Myles, but he hesitated. The urge to smoke was too great and he couldn't resist the temptation.

"Aren't you cigarette-free until your teeth heal?" Hayden reminded Myles.

"To hell with it," Myles brought out his lighter. "I need a smoke."

Anderson calmed down, breathing out a large puff. "So Cooper, got any family members that live around here?"

"Yeah, my Ma and Pa are on the other side of town." Cooper took a sip of his beverage. "I take care of them every now and then to make sure they're alright."

"Any relatives?" Anderson went on.

Cooper sighed. "Yeah, three older brothers, but they want nothing to do with me."

"Why's that?" Myles asked.

The look on Cooper's face made him appear humbled by the conversation. "Eh, they've got their own lives to take care of. They're all way older than me. They've got some pretty big jobs too."

"Tell me," Williams cut into the conversation with a slightly sarcastic tone. "Why did you go into law enforcement?"

Cooper shrugged. "I guess I just saw the movies and thought it was cool."

Hayden interrupted, joking around. "Still think it's cool?" referring to how beat up he looked.

Cooper looked around. "As long as I'm not paying for this meal, I'm completely fine with whatever this job throws at me." The table laughed before Cooper continued. "What about you Williams? Why did you join the force?"

"I wanted to help people, duh." Williams and the others could be intimidating at times, but Myles enjoyed it most when they were off their shift where they could just relax and unload.

Cooper turned to Myles. "I'm really curious to know; I've asked Karter this too; what's the craziest cop story you've experienced?"

Myles' eyebrows raised as he dug deep in his memory to think of a story. "Uhh... I'd probably have to say when I was stabbed twice in the stomach."

Cooper's eyes opened up. "You were stabbed? What happened?"

It pleased Myles to know Cooper was so interested in the stories he had to tell. Myles sat back in his chair, getting comfortable to unleash the tale he had to tell. "Well...

"It was probably last year or the year before that; I received a call on some guy who was really making people nervous. At some apartment, a man was apparently walking around, threatening to hurt the neighbors. When I arrived there, the fellow was on the third floor, shouting at a manager. When I saw the guy, he was a nervous wreck. My guess is that he was trying to commit suicide by cop.

"'Put the knife down!' I screamed, pointing my taser at the dude.

"'Shoot me! Kill me!' he kept repeating as he got closer.

"As much as I feared for my life, I didn't want to kill this guy. The man lunged at me when I least expected it and shanked me twice. That's when I dry tasered him. That's where I got these:" Myles lifted up his shirt to show two scars near the sides of his abdominal region. "They weren't really deep. The kid was scared."

Williams sighed. "Yet another story of Myles being reckless about his life. Any other smart cop would've tased him before he even got the chance to lunge."

"Didn't you have any body armor on?" Cooper inquired. "I mean, isn't that a must have when up against a guy like that?"

"I did have body armor on," Myles claimed. "It just went perfectly between the platings. He shanked me three times before I got him down. It's just two of those actually got through."

"That seems rough..." Cooper looked around. "Does anyone think they can top that? What about you Williams? Any good stories?"

Williams thought for a moment, drawing a blank. "I really can't think of a time that I was injured as much as Myles. I've been a little bit smarter," he joked. "I think the craziest thing I've seen though has to be was when Myles got in that crazy car wreck."

Myles groaned. "Ahh, I forgot about that."

Williams continued, "Now it's my time to tell a story."

"Just like Cooper, Myles almost got himself killed because of poor judgment on my behalf. We were on a car chase, and a robbery had just occurred. It might've been a bank, or it might've been a 7/11 gas station; I can't remember. Anyways, me, Hayden, and Myles were all in pursuit, right? We decided to try bumping the robber's car off the road into some bushes outside of the city. I was behind, so it was all up to Hayden and Myles. Hayden bumped the car, but he swerved directly into Myles, making him roll over like six times.

"'Myles!' I screamed, but I got no response. 'I don't know where all this blood is coming from... It's just everywhere... I can't see a cut...'

"'Get him out of the car!' Hayden screamed with his gun drawn at the robber's car. 'Lay him flat on the ground! Get some water from the trunk of my car and wash the blood off!'

"I spent forever trying to find where the cut came from, but it just happened to be a small cut on his head that bled like hell."

Myles rubbed his forehead. "And people ask how I have so many health problems."

Cooper was intrigued. "Any other close death experiences you've had that you'd like to share with us, Myles?"

"Nope," Myles spoke bluntly, but in a joking way. "I have a feeling though that you're gonna do the same."

Cooper laughed. "Yeah right." He looked to Anderson. "What about you sir? Scariest moment?"

Anderson thought out loud. "Scariest moment, huh? I suppose the time I defused a bomb was pretty exciting.

"This was after Williams became an officer. I was called down to the center of the city by my commanding officer on the case of some bomb that was planted. It was supposed to take out a whole group of rich people, but someone reported seeing a lost briefcase to the police. Of course, I wasn't the one defusing the bomb, I was simply trying to clear the building of any civilians. I was armed with an assault rifle and everything. It was definitely something I'll never forget."

"Did they ever find the person who planted the bomb?" Cooper inquired.

"I can't remember; it's been so long since it's happened." Anderson smiled. "What about you, Cooper? Any cool patrol stories?"

"Hell no." Cooper laughed before turning to the only one left that hadn't shared a story. "What about you Hayden? Any stories to tell? Maybe some really cool story about how you got that scar on the side of your head?"

Hayden seemed a little offended. "I got the scar before I went on the force. Besides, I don't have all these tall tales like Myles and Williams. Don't listen to a dang story they tell you. I bet at least one of those stories are exaggerated."

Myles puffed out a smoke cloud. "You're just jealous you don't have a good story to tell."

"Pfft, I got stories," Hayden bluffed.

"Alright then, go ahead," Myles spoke sarcastically.

Hayden cleared his throat before starting. "This might not be an exciting story, but it's sure one that spooks me. This story has no exaggeration what so ever...

"One case upon a time, I was called to help out some woman that felt like she was being watched. She said she's been noticing a guy at her window when she'd come downstairs. She was never really able to get someone down there in time to get him, so the police decided to send me down there in a patrol vehicle to watch her house at night until they caught the stalker.

"I must've spaced out for a moment and was checking my MDT; I didn't notice the man standing at my passenger door, staring straight at me. Once I finally saw him, he had a big smile on his face... It was almost like he was glad to see me. He was quite a skinny, scrawny man. Still... Something about the way he walked just gave me shivers... I asked for his name, but he just kept mumbling gibberish. Eventually, I started understanding what he was saying.

"'That young lady in that house over there,' he said. 'She's in danger.'

"'What do you mean?' I asked him. 'Why is she in danger?'

"'Well... Every night she forgets to lock her back door... It's way too easy to get in, and she really does have soft skin. I'd hate for someone to come in and use her...'

"At that moment I was just creeped out. I arrested the man, told the girl to start locking her doors before she slept, and she never experienced anything of that matter after that. Of course, I never shared to her what really happened."

Myles started laughing sarcastically. "You made that up. You hypocrite; it's fake."

Hayden shook his head. "I swear on my life that happened."

Cooper shivered. "It certainly made the hair on the back of my neck stand up," he admitted.

As Hayden and Myles went back and forth about their stories, and which one was the best, a waiter came by to deliver the food. Their rambling stopped there as they started to stuff their face with "the best Chinese food in the state."

ELEVEN

PURSUIT

Andrew Sutton lived in an apartment within the impecunious part of town. He was the man dealers went to for narcotics; he would cook them up and sell them off to people like Erik. Andrew was allegedly part of The Aesthetics and was considered a very high target. He actually worked side by side with the one calling the shots in the gang, which made him a very important asset.

Andrew was known to have many different addresses because he moved around frequently. This made things very difficult for the detectives to go in to question him. Luckily, Myles was able to pinpoint where he lived at the moment through thorough research. An officer made sure to do some reconnaissance on Andrew so that when the time came, other officers would be able to make a move on him. Those officers happened to be Myles and Hayden. They both got out of their vehicles, making their way to the apartment complex.

"So why couldn't Cooper come?" Hayden inquired.

Myles sighed. "He's got some other stuff to do

now since he doesn't work in my office anymore. Plus, this may get really dangerous really fast." Myles could actually articulately talk now; the swelling in his mouth went down a little, and just left with a darkish bruise.

Hayden patted Myles' back. "It's never easy to watch over a recruit and do your job at the same time. What happened to him wasn't any of your fault," Hayden reassured.

"I know..." Myles looked down. "I'm still responsible for it though."

"Hey," Hayden changed the subject, holding out his fist. "Just like old times? Just the two of us?"

Myles half smiled before fist bumping Hayden lightly. "Just like old times," he repeated.

Myles and Hayden made their way up the stairs of the apartment to the second floor; the floor Andrew was known to live on. As they approach his room number, they started to keep quiet. Myles put his ear against the door, hearing audio from a TV.

"Well, someone is inside." Myles started to knock on the door a few times with the bottom of his fist.

After a while of waiting, the door opened and a face appeared. Hayden stepped forward. "We're part of the PCP—" Before he could finish, the man shut the door in their face; seeming frightened by the two cops.

Myles looked to Hayden. "Well, that was him." Myles knocked on the door a few times again to get Andrew's attention.

The door seemed to be broken in some way, so as Myles knocked, it opened up. As the door slowly creaked open, Andrew was revealed climbing out of his window.

"Stop!" Hayden yelled as he ran for the window.

Before Hayden got to Andrew, he had already

fallen on some soft shrubs from the story below him. The detectives started to climb out of the second-floor window just as Andrew did, and bolted after the avoiding criminal. Hayden pointed towards Andrew's direction, who was running on top of cars, attempting to get away.

"Stop!" Hayden screamed again, slowly losing his stamina. "Stop or you will be tased!"

The two detectives were mere yards away from the criminal, but he showed no sign of stopping. He actually seemed as though he was getting faster, and Myles felt as though they were going to lose him.

"Stop, or I will shoot you!" Hayden screamed with his last full breath of air.

Myles was a little more ahead than Hayden at the time. Myles glanced back to see Hayden pulling out his sidearm and pointing it at the running man. Myles' eyes opened wide; Hayden pulled the trigger, but to Hayden's surprise, there wasn't a round in the chamber. Hayden then started to cock the slide back so the gun could fire.

"No!" Myles screamed as he grabbed Hayden's arm, pressing the mag release on Hayden's pistol, dropping it onto the ground. In one swift move, he pulled the slide of Hayden's gun back, popping the bullet back out of the chamber before Hayden was able to fire the weapon.

While Hayden paused, struggling to catch his breath as he reached down for his magazine, Myles made his last push towards Andrew. His long legs took wide strides, slowly getting closer. Andrew started to lose his breath; Myles, on the other hand, was fighting his bad lungs to get a good breath of fresh air to run. With one last push, Myles lunged towards Andrew, tackling him to the hard concrete. Both of them were winded, hyperventilating on the ground.

Though quite on the verge of vomiting, Myles tried grabbing Andrew's wrists, pulling them behind his back to handcuff him.

"Give me your hands!" Myles shouted. "Stop resisting!"

"Let me go!" Andrew howled breathlessly.

There was a loud and distinct clicking made from the handcuffs Myles placed on Andrew. He kept a knee on Andrew's shoulders to keep him from getting up. Hayden finally caught up to the two, putting his gun back in the holster.

"Should've shot the bastard..." Hayden mumbled under his breath.

Myles still couldn't believe that Hayden almost shot a person because they were running away. He noticed blood coming from the suspect. He must've been scrapped up pretty bad from the tumble; even his shirt was ripped up.

"Why'd you run from us?" Myles inquired.

Andrew wheezed through his ragged breathing. "You said you'd shoot me if I kept running! What are you talking about! How was I supposed to act!"

Myles looked up at Hayden and gave him a glare before looking back down to Andrew. "You were running away before we said that. Why did you run from us?"

"I don't know..." Andrew struggled to break free. "You guys looked like bounty hunters or assassins or something. I was just protecting myself."

Myles started to search Andrew for weapons and drugs but found nothing else but a lighter. "Well if you would've listened to me, you'd hear that we are part of the police. Now, let's start this all over. Hello, we are part of the PCPD. Do you happen to be Andrew?"

"What does it look like to you?" Andrew snapped.

Myles felt too irritated for the smart remarks but maintained composure. "Alright, get on your side and tuck your knees to your chest." After Andrew did as he was told, Myles pulled him onto his knees. "Now stand up."

Myles took Andrew to his car, where he sat him down on the side of the curb. Myles was surprised when he saw that Andrew's hands were blood red from the tumble on the concrete. He put on some rubber disposable gloves and grabbed a medical baggy from his car. Hayden seemed disgusted by Myles' considerate gesture.

"Would you like some water?" Myles politely asked Andrew. Andrew nodded.

"What are you doing?" Hayden hissed.

"I'm giving him water," Myles bluntly stated.

Hayden stepped towards Myles. "But he's a criminal!"

"He's a human being." Myles stood up to Hayden, looking down at him. There was some silence between the two as they exchanged some heated looks. Myles broke away from the glance and went behind Andrew, removing his cuffs.

This set Hayden off. "What do you think you're doing!" Hayden spoke lividly.

Myles tried being as careful as he could when removing the handcuffs, as not to hurt Andrew. "I can't clean up his hands if they're behind him."

Hayden was silent for a moment before he spoke. "You're really putting the two of us in danger."

"Whose side are you on?" Myles argued. "We're here to protect Andrew and the other gang members from meeting some psychopath, and you're here trying to shoot him! He just ran! He's not even a possible suspect! He's a possible victim!"

Hayden clenched his fists. "He could've had a gun! You could've gotten shot! What if he got away?"

Myles swept the hair from his face. "Well he's caught right now, isn't he? I really don't think he could take two cops down with only a lighter either. I don't see what's gotten into you lately, but I don't like it..." Myles got up and grabbed a water bottle from a pack in his trunk.

Hayden had pure disappointment in his eyes. "I really thought you were better than this Myles. You use to have such great potential. Now I can't even trust you without the possibility of being put in danger by you. Williams was right; you trust people way too easily." Hayden turned and walked away, but before leaving he got one last jab at Myles. "This is probably why Cooper almost got killed."

Myles tried not to take it personally, but he couldn't help it. Hayden was his best friend, and they never fought like this. He went back to Andrew and kneeled down with a water bottle at hand. Since Andrew's hands were bloody, Myles helped him out by holding the bottle as he drank.

"Your partner really seems like a crooked cop," Andrew coldly stated.

Myles sighed. "He has his moments. I really didn't expect him to threaten to shoot you though... There's nothing you had to worry about; it's not like him to do that." Myles put a cap on his water bottle, reaching into his little baggy of medical supplies, pulling out some gauze. "Now let me see your hands."

Andrew was surprised. "Why are you helping me?"

Myles shrugged. "Well that's what I'm here to do, right? Help people? Besides, I don't want you bleeding all over the back seat of my car," he joked. "Now watch out, this might sting." Myles poured some hydrogen peroxide on a cotton ball, which he then dabbed against Andrew's cuts. Once finished, he started to bandage up his scrapes.

"Thanks..." Andrew seemed reluctant to say. "I've never met a cop before that's willing to help someone like this."

That statement made Myles worried. "Yeah, I really wish that wasn't the case. We already get a bad rep as it is." He looked around seeing that the whole situation was grabbing a lot of people's attention. Myles didn't feel safe interrogating Andrew in the parking lot, so he decided he was going to bring him to the department. "You have the right to remain silent. Anything you say can and will be used against you in a court of law. You have the right to an attorney. If you cannot afford an attorney, one will be provided for you. Do you understand the rights I have just read to you?" Myles waited until Andrew nodded before continuing. "With these rights in mind, do you wish to speak to me?"

Andrew was a little confused about what this meant. He only knew that cops usually read this to him when he was being arrested. "Um... Yes."

Myles had left to go get some lunch. He brought a bag with him to the interrogation cavity of the department.

He saw through the one-sided window into the room to find Hayden still talking to Andrew. Hayden appeared to be wrapping up though; he appeared to be frustrated with the subject. Hayden finally got up and went out the door. He didn't pay much attention to Myles; ignoring him. Apparently, he still hadn't gotten over their little fuss before. Myles didn't worry though; he'd learned to just give him time.

Hayden turned to another cop. "He won't talk. He's not budging whatsoever. I think we should just release him."

Myles stepped forward. "Give me a chance to talk with the guy. I'm sure we can at least get something out of him."

Hayden was silent, and barely looked up to Myles, so Myles simply took the initiative and walked inside with a bag of his lunch.

"Good evening." Myles sat down at a table next to the wall; Andrew sat adjacent to which.

"What's that?" Andrew pointed to the brown bag, which smelt like greasy foods.

Myles shrugged, starting to unload the brown bag. "Some lunch I just picked up. I figured you were hungry."

Myles grabbed some food out of the bag, then giving the rest to Andrew. Andrew looked inside to find a burger with some fries, ketchup packets, and a few brown unused napkins.

Andrew seemed a bit suspicious. "What's this for? Why are you being so polite to me? If it's to get me to talk, it ain't gonna happen."

Myles looked confused. "You don't have to worry about it. I'm just here to talk to you about whatever you're willing and able to tell. I wouldn't consider you a criminal, so I'm not going to treat you like one."

"I certainly feel like a criminal." Andrew took a bite out of his hamburger and spoke while he chewed. "Did you see the way your partner was talking to me? I was put in a dirty cell too for a while. If this is how you treat normal people, then I don't ever want to run into you on the wrong side."

Myles swatted his hand before swallowing a mouthful of fries. "My partner was trying to pin something on you that you didn't do; luckily you have me. I just said you got scared and thought we were trying to kill you. I want you to get out as soon as you can so I can get back to my job. I don't know why my partner is being such a sore ass about it. I guess he just didn't like the way you first looked at us."

Andrew seemed to have taken the fact of the matter seriously. "I wouldn't trust your partner if I were you. Seems sketchy."

"Don't worry. Even if I wasn't here, he probably wouldn't be able to place anything on you. It's not that easy to get charged with something. Your individual rights protect you from that."

"Don't you guys have body cameras or something?" Andrew inquired.

Myles took a sip of his drink before continuing. "Not unless we know something may go down. We're detectives, so we're not expected to wear it 24-7. Plus the information on those cameras may release very important information that we're not ready to disclose; not to mention it blows our cover."

"That's pretty frightening..." Andrew rubbed the

back of his arm. "So why am I here to begin with? Am I dismissed yet?"

"Not yet." Myles shook his head. "All I need to know is information. Anything you have. The smallest bit of it will help us out immensely."

"Blackmail! I knew this is why you got me food!" Andrew cried out.

Myles started speaking in a stern tone. "Listen, Andrew, I want to help you. Right now you may be in danger, and I'm trying to find the one responsible for killing your friends. If you don't tell me, you and the rest of your friends could get hurt. Please let me do my job and you do yours."

Andrew shifted in his seat, continuing to stuff his mouth with fast food. He paused and considered listening to what Myles had to say.

"Please be completely honest with me." Myles' tone started to ease again. "Do you happen to know a man named Owen Reid?"

Andrew seemed unsure. "What's he look like?"

"Short blonde hair, green eyes. He's a little scrawny too. Around 5'6; any of it ring a bell?"

Andrew shook his head. "I'm sure I've seen someone like that before, but I personally don't know anyone like that."

"Do you have any idea who could be doing this to you and your friends?"

Andrew was silent for a moment. Myles caught his eyes shift before he spoke. "No, I don't."

"You don't sound completely oblivious," Myles noted.

"I'm being honest," Andrew claimed.

"Who do you work for? Do you know anyone else that might be in danger?" Myles shifted forward.

"I work for my boss." Andrew paused. "You really shouldn't get mixed up in this. The boss doesn't like it when people get caught up in his business. He'll make sure to get back at you if you keep going with this whole investigation thing. We can handle it ourselves; just take your hands off."

Myles slammed the palm of his hand down on the table. "Dammit Andrew, you and everyone you know are in danger. I just need names. Tell me something I don't know."

Andrew, starting to feel intimidated, caved in and let out a piece of information. "After what had happened between the police and The Sin a couple of days ago, there has been a lot of tension between us and them; it's all thanks to you. If you absolutely have to know, try Phillip Hardy. He's the next best thing to the boss himself. He's the boss man's personal bodyguard." Starting to look defeated, "If you tell a single soul, there will be hell to pay. They're safe as long as their identities are protected. If there's some sort of shootout between us, their blood is on your hands."

Myles shifted back into the chair and wiped the hair from his face. "I just want to catch the killer. I'm trying to do it as cautiously as I can because I know how much danger I can put you through if I'm not. If you help me, you can guide me through so I don't make any wrong turns."

Andrew shrugged. "I guess... But I'll only help you; no one else. Come alone to my apartment whenever you plan on doing something. You have to agree to never do something unless I give you the signal. Otherwise, no deal."

Myles rubbed his chin, deciding whether or not he should take the deal. "If it's for your safety and the safety of others, then I'll do it."

"Good," Andrew let out a sigh of relief. "Can I leave now? This place is depressing."

Myles rubbed his face exhaustedly. "Go ahead..." Myles felt beat; laying his head down on his hand. Andrew grabbed the rest of his food and left the room.

TWELVE

NUMBERS

Myles sat on a stool in his lab, playing with the little chess piece that was found from Eric's crime scene. The Knight piece itself was of a chrome, shining black color. He thought to himself in silence, pondering what was around him. He needed time to think, and there was no better spot than his own workplace. Everyone seemed to be on edge lately and Myles didn't completely know why. It was quite stressful, but he was determined to figure it out. He recollected his thoughts and what he knew about the murders, laying it out in front of him on a table. With a gloved hand, he handled the pieces of evidence; he gently pressed his thumb down on the mane of the knight piece.

"Could I just be misguided?" Myles thought as he considered the possibility of Owen Reid being the main suspect. It seemed way too coincidental; the note, the scuff of hair found at the crime scene. There wasn't enough evidence though. All that could be found were these stray chess pieces. Were they really just a signature? Or could they be some sort of leverage Myles could use against the killer? Myles thought about the possibility that this "Boss man" could be the culprit. It may be just some crazy conspiracy, but what if the boss was trying to cut off some loose ends? There were way too many possibilities and not enough evidence. No phone call from Owen's neighbor, no blood samples or weapons found, no pointers, nothing else to work with.

As Myles thought to himself, his thumb started to turn the Knight with his fingers. This led to a loud squeak being heard. At first, it startled him, but he then realized that the knight piece wasn't just one product. Upon closer inspection, he observed a barely noticeable line across the base of the knight. Myles continued turning it, but it didn't seem to open. Perhaps it's not threaded? He kept turning the base over and over again. Eventually, he heard a click as the piece lay flat upside down; the base would no longer twist clockwise. After rotating the base counterclockwise, the base clicked again, allowing the whole bottom half of the piece to come off. It was simply held together by a pin, and two different thread linings; using gravity to his advantage, Myles was able to keep the pins down.

After admiring the design, Myles noticed that there was a cavity inside the chess piece, housing a tightly rolled up piece of paper. Shocked and eager to find more, Myles unrolled the message, finding what seemed to be numbers on it. "14-43-44-64-43-11-32-13-33..." Myles read the first set of numbers. "32-31..." Then the next, followed by "62-15-64-15-33-61-15." Myles damned his luck. Finally some sort of puzzle; some sort of sign. The only problem was that this was intentional. These numbers could mean anything too; there's no positive answer to this. Why was this left behind? Why was this created? Myles repeated the numbers out loud and in his head, trying to think of a plausible answer to the riddle. He first started counting numbers in the alphabet; to which nothing made sense. He then looked it up, trying to see if it had some relevance on the internet, but it was revealed to be another disappointment. He then tried researching dates that might've been related to the individuals that were murdered; nothing made sense, and even if it was, it wasn't recorded on any enforcement database.

Myles paced the floor, repeating the numbers in his head: "64-15-33-61-15..." There didn't seem to be a pattern at all. Myles tried turning the numbers upside down, reading it through a mirror, backward, sideways, nothing seemed to click. "Maybe there could be a clue somewhere in the past evidence we've found?" he thought as he looked through the pictures on the table in front of him. A certain picture, in particular, caught his eye. "Those yond sineth shalt meeteth grievance..." The picture showed the bloody writing on the walls of Erik's scene. The more Myles thought about it, the more that made sense. He ripped a piece of paper off some diagnostics paper he found and started jotting down the numbers matched with the writing on the wall. Maybe the numbers were letters? No... that didn't seem to spell anything. It then clicked; what if the first number was the word, and the second number was the letter? Myles tried this formula out to see if any dots connected.

"14-43-44-64-43-11-32-13-33," the first set of numbers. "First word... fourth letter..." Myles spoke to himself. "S... a... l... v... a... t... i... o... n... Salvation..." A genuine smile peaked across Myles' face. He had figured out the formula. Myles double checked himself

before going on to the next set of numbers. "32-31...
i... s... is... Salvation is..." Myles triple checked himself
before going on to the last set of numbers. "62-15-64-
15-33-61-15... r... e... v... e... n... g... e... revenge...
Salvation is revenge." Myles looked puzzled. What did
this mean? How could Myles apply this to what he
already knew? Though unsure, Myles knew it was a
massive leap into the correct direction. The more he
thought about it, the more he realized that the writing
on the wall didn't make much sense considering the
background of those in other gangs. Now he knew one
of the leading reasons for the death of Erik Vincent:
revenge.

Now that Myles was aware of how important these
chess pieces were, he couldn't resist turning down the
opportunity to find out more through the pawn. He held
up the piece and studied it carefully; the craftsmanship
was truly commendable. He noticed right away that
no matter how hard he tried, the base would not turn.
He started to inspect the piece's biggest characteristics;
poking different places, twisting it, letting it sit on certain
angles, shaking it, tapping it. Eventually, after twisting
hard enough, he unscrewed the head of the pawn off,
exposing threads. After fiddling with it some more,
Myles twisted the threads the other direction, eventually
unscrewing the threads themselves, exposing what
seemed to be a double-sided screw. Upon examining the
inside of the head, he noticed a different set of threads;
what was also very obvious was the length difference of
each side of the double-sided screw. This gave Myles the
impression to switch the screw and tighten it back on.
After doing so, there was a click, and the bottom of the
pawn piece fell open.

The machining on this was stunning at least, and showed no sign of gaps whatsoever, surprising the detective. By turning the screw around and using the longest end, it pushed a little pin, which allowed the bottom section of the pawn fall. Inside this brilliant puzzle was yet another strip of tightly rolled paper; this time it was a few sentences. The note read "it's never whAt you expect it t0 be. the ones delighted By the suffering of others sHall meet the same demise. indulGenCe is paid with death."

Myles immediately noticed the capital letters that were misplaced throughout the note. He decided to write this out. The letters together read "AOBHGC." Obviously, this didn't spell a word, but maybe it could spell something else. Myles was intrigued, knowing he may be able to decipher the puzzle.

Cooper had been checking all around campus for Myles. He wasn't in his office, so Cooper assumed he was in the lab.

"Myles?" Cooper peeked his head in; the black eye and bruises had gone away, leaving a light shade around his eyes and mouth.

Myles was startled by the sudden vocalized sound. He turned back seeing Cooper by the door. "I think I've cracked it!"

Cooper looked confused; Myles was tired and didn't speak clearly. "Cracked what?"

"The chess pieces have messages!" Myles grabbed hold of Cooper's shoulders and shook him back and forth. "The knight had numbers which read 'salvation is revenge.' The pawn just gave me a few letters, but it's numbers! It's a date!"

Myles was talking too fast, and Cooper couldn't keep up. "How do you know?"

Myles let go of Cooper and started to show off the slip of paper he found in the pawn. "The letters I got was AO-BH-GC. The letters correspond with numbers based on the alphabet! A is the first letter of the alphabet so it would be 1. O would normally be 15, which didn't make sense until I realized I should have interpreted the O as a zero! B is 2, H is 8, G is 7, and C is 3! All together based on the sentences it's found in, you get 10-28-73! It's a date! October 28th, 2073! This could be another clue we can ask around about. Andrew could possibly know; we have to get to him!"

Cooper still had a face of pure confusion, but Myles was so eager to find out what it meant that he was basically pushing Cooper out of the lab.

On the way to Andrew's apartment, the sun had already gone down; traffic still boomed as it always did on the highways. A day or two had passed since Myles spoke to Andrew, so he'd consider this a step in the right direction. Cooper followed Myles up to Andrew's apartment room; this time Myles wasn't expecting to chase after someone, and he definitely didn't expect Cooper to almost shoot the suspect. The feeling of Déjà vu came to Myles as he knocked on his door.

"PCPD!" Myles hollered, but with no reply.

Cooper turned to Myles "Do you think he's just not home?"

"Well, his car was here." Myles put his ear up to the door, hearing a TV from inside. "Someone is inside; the TV is on." He knocked again.

There was no answer like before, and the detectives

were getting a little impatient; though Myles knew there was nothing he could do about it. Maybe it was just a bad time.

"I guess we could just check back later," Myles sighed, starting to feel too curious for his own good.

Myles and Cooper made their way back to the car, defeated. Andrew's window overlooked the parking lot, and from what Myles could tell, the lights were on.

Myles looked back, making a fuss about how he didn't answer the door. "His lights are on! He couldn't have left, right? Who leaves their lights o…" Myles paused, looking at Andrew's window from across the parking lot.

Cooper turned to Myles, anticipating him to go on. "What?" Cooper glanced to wherever Myles was focusing on.

Myles walked closer to the apartments, keeping his eyes on Andrew's window. Eventually, Myles was close enough to clearly see exactly what was through his window. His face dropped immediately to pure dread; he could practically feel his eyes start to water out of pure frustration. Cooper soon noticed exactly what caught Myles' attention, placing a hand over his mouth.

"We were too late…" Myles uttered.

THIRTEEN

NOOSE

It's never what you expect it to be. The ones delighted by the suffering of others shall meet the same demise. Indulgence is paid with death. Andrew Sutton was murdered, or so it seemed. Hanging from a noose with his cheeks sliced from ear to ear, giving the appearance of a crooked smile. In front of him was nothing more than a black queen piece. "I'm sorry," was smeared on the walls with blood. The plea for forgiveness could be seen from outside Andrew's window, alongside the hanging body.

"Damn... What a sight," Williams mumbled to himself.

Myles' heart was beating through his chest. "The blood's still red, and the muscles are stiff; it's going through the process of rigor mortis. I'd say we're not far off from seeing him die; he definitely died before we showed up though."

Cooper looked like he'd never seen a dead body so mutilated before; so decomposed. It made it all so unreal. "Is it suicide or murder?" He could barely come close to the body without gagging, much less look at it.

"That's what we're trying to figure out," Hayden declared looking under beds and couches.

Williams was sketching the crime scene down on a piece of paper. "Is it just me, or does it look like Andrew is our real killer?" Williams remarked.

Hayden nodded. "That might be the case. Look what I found here. A whole case of chess pieces. They all look like the ones left with Erik and Jonathan."

Cooper examined them carefully. "They sure do." He paused before going on. "And there's a black knight, pawn, and queen missing. The question remains: why did he do it?"

"Guilt," Hayden answered. "He must've been out of his mind. Killed Erik and Jonathan; two people he was very close to. After we interrogated him, he must've gotten nervous and killed himself. Not before cutting a crooked smile into his face and writing 'sorry' on the wall."

Cooper shivered. "What an agonizing way to go out..."

"It makes sense though," Williams noted.

Myles rubbed his chin. "What if he was murdered, and all of this was just a way for the killer to hide his tracks?"

"That may be," Williams thought out loud. "There's no evidence backing it up though," he countered.

"It all makes sense though," Hayden remarked. "The guy was a nut job, so he killed the people worked beside. This would explain why the other gang members knew nothing about it. It's just gang drama."

Myles checked under blankets, couch cushions and

carpets for any other clues as he spoke. "But what about the note left at Owen's house?" Myles brought up.

"Might've just been a coincidence," Williams shrugged. "I don't know. Maybe there's more than one killer. Maybe this could've been assisted suicide. If this is true, this individual is still yet to be known."

"What about the murder weapons?" Myles pressed. "Unless he threw them out somewhere, we're not completely positive that this could be him."

Cooper crossed the room, inspecting the kitchen filled with dirty plates and trash. "Maybe there's still more to uncover."

Myles scanned through calendars and cabinets. "We may know his intention on killing them, but we still don't know what the date meant."

"What date?" Williams questioned.

"The date in the pawn piece," Myles forgot to mention. "It had a date in it. It was a past date, but it's anniversary was coming up pretty soon."

Williams finished sketching the scene out on paper, continuing to check the perimeter of the apartment room. "Maybe we can call Phillip Hardy up to get some kind of insight on why this happened. This could be the real deal breaker here."

Myles reached forward with a gloved hand and grabbed the queen piece off the table. The detectives already took pictures of the crime scene, so now they were just grabbing evidence. Myles started studying the queen piece carefully.

"What are you doing?" Sergeant Williams inquired.

Instead of answering Williams' question verbally, he decided to show him what he was doing through his discoveries. The four gathered around in a circle. Myles tried twisting and turning parts of the queen, but to no avail. The three other detectives began doubting Myles and his capabilities with unbalanced looks; Myles was genuinely puzzled but intrigued. Myles started to shake the chess piece, hoping to hear something inside. To his surprise, there was a rather distinct click when he shook it horizontally.

The head of the queen started to unscrew; revealing a needle-like key. It had seemed that there was a pin that was held in by a magnet, which was keeping the head from being unscrewed. The only way to release the pin was to forcefully shake it to one side. Now that the needle was revealed, Myles needed to find a way to use it. Now that the queen's crown was off, the little nob below the head would unscrew; it was almost like a washer. Under this washer like nob was a pinhole, which resembled the shape of the key.

Fitting the needle in, there was a final click followed by the puzzle piece falling apart completely, uncovering a note. Had the washer like nob not been there, the pin would release the puzzle. Since the nob acted as a guard, the pin never pressed into the lock. The lock was simply held together by springs; once it was engaged, it all would fall apart.

Cooper seemed to admire Myles. "What a way to hide a message…"

Williams picked up the message and started to read it. "It says… I did it." Williams then showed the note to the rest of the detectives; written in scribbled pencil, it'd definitely be believable if Andrew was the real culprit. "I think we know who did it now."

Myles shook his head. "It could have easily been

planted there by the murderer so that they could get away."

Williams began to retrieve a plastic baggy, which he then placed the pieces to the puzzle inside. "Before we start to lay this case to rest, we should just get some insight from another member of the gang. I'm sure it'll all make sense after we talk to them." Williams then started to look through Andrew's belongings.

Myles was disappointed by this sudden end in the investigation. He worked so hard to find the killer and bring justice to the ones that were murdered. Instead, it was abruptly extinguished so hopelessly, so unsatisfyingly, so unforgiving. The thought that Myles was so close to cracking down on Andrew made his stomach turn. There was really nothing the detectives could do but clean up the mess.

"The queen I think makes the most sense," Hayden commented. "The queen is the most powerful piece on the board. It has the power to control and manipulate, exactly as he was doing with us the whole time. He put us out on a wild chase, and the clues he left just threw us off. The queen is hidden behind the pawns and knights and bishops but isn't afraid of doing the dirty work. When put under the stress of being caught, he just gave up."

"Guess we finally cracked it," Cooper declared. "Don't worry Myles. There was nothing we could've done for him. We did the best we could."

Myles started to piece everything together the best he could from what he knew. Andrew was a nutcase that killed his friends. From the clues and hints left behind, Andrew did it because of revenge. How far could he have gotten if the detectives didn't get involved is unknown, but Myles didn't want to think about that. The only thing that Myles didn't understand was that Andrew didn't seem unstable; he looked completely normal. Even if he did throw away the weapons he used to kill Erik and Jonathan, the things written in the clues were very unexpected from a person like Andrew.

Another thing that didn't add up was where Owen Reid came into play. Was it really a coincidence that he was just involved in this whole dilemma? Even then, what was the reason for the note being left in the chicken pen? Was that a coincidence too? It was only a tuft of hair found at Erik's crime scene that gave the detectives the impression that he was involved. Could it be that Andrew knew about it, and planned on pinning it on him so it would throw off the investigation? Though that made sense, it wouldn't explain how Andrew knew exactly what the detectives were thinking.

Nothing was stopping Myles of believing Andrew had killed Owen in his own home; that would further back up that Andrew did it all. It would explain Owen going missing, and why his lights were on when Myles was visiting his house. The detectives never did receive a call from Owen's neighbor. Even with all this backing up Andrew as the murderer, it still would've been much easier for the real killer to simply pin it all against Andrew in this simple scene.

Then it hit Myles; one very important detail that would prove whether or not Andrew was the killer. He started to lift Andrew's pants and sleeves.

"What are you doing Myles?" Williams inquired.

Myles was determined. "I'm checking his body for any scars."

The connection never made it through to Williams. "What scars? Why would you be looking for scars?"

Myles looked back to Williams. "As far as we know from the scene at Jonathan's death, the murderer was stabbed in the leg with a glass shard, right? If we can actually find that scar somewhere on his body, then we'll know for sure that Andrew was the killer; at least that he murdered Jonathan. As far as I can tell, there are no scars."

Williams considered the thought. "Unless we have it all wrong, this may be the knocking blow." Williams appeared to be relieved that there was one little piece of evidence they can hold on to. "It may not prove that Andrew is innocent, but it may prove that there is another person we have not caught yet."

It may have been the best thing that has shown up at this crime scene. There was no other reasonable explanation for the missing piece of glass.

Myles paced the floor slowly. "There was no other cuts or abrasions on Andrew's body besides the ones that killed him. The only blood in the room was the puddle under him, which meant he cut the smile into his face right before he hung himself. If that were the case, why is it that there's no weapon on the floor beside him?" Myles observed.

Williams was dumbfounded. "Maybe it was staged after all... There are a lot of things in this room that are sharp, but none of them are bloody."

Hayden started to look less confident about his theory. "Hmm... Good point... Maybe it could've been assisted suicide?"

Myles shook his head. "Why would the person

assisting him keep the blade? Plus, this is an awful way to assist suicide."

Myles was glad he now found a way to gain some sort of leverage against the thought that Andrew was the murderer. This proved that the investigation was not over, and there was still more to it.

Cooper smirked. "Well, now we have our first staged suicide. We must be treading on the killer's toes."

"Now we know Andrew was murdered," Williams stated. "This puts a lot off of Andrew being the culprit. I guess the only thing we can do from here is to keep asking questions until we find our murderer."

"We could start with Phillip," Myles mentioned. "We have a lot of questions now, and I'm sure he'll have it."

Williams intervened with a thought. "Now that we have a constantly recurring theme with these deaths, we may be able to have 24-7 surveillance on the rest of the group if we get their permission so that they remain safe until we catch our killer."

FOURTEEN

THE BISHOP

Time is a very important asset for detectives; without it, the investigation would fall apart. Unfortunately for Myles, Hayden, Sergeant Williams, and Cooper, time was running out. The danger others were in was solely based on how much time the detectives would waste. Phillip Hardy was hard to find, like everyone else that had been killed. How this killer remained a step ahead was unknown, but the detectives knew that they had to stop the unknown murderer from taking more lives.

Williams wanted to provide protection to Phillip, but at the same time, he needed answers. Williams positioned Myles, Cooper, and Hayden nearby to come in if needed. It was quite dark by this time, and a full moon was out. Williams decided the best approach was to get ahold of him on his own. Williams didn't know whether to come looking like a cop or incognito as a civilian to lower suspicion. If he came as an officer, Phillip could run or become very defensive; if he came as a civilian, Phillip might not even answer the door, or worse, think that Williams was from a gang. There was no easy choice, so Williams presented himself in a normal jacket with his gear underneath.

Williams arrived in his unmarked car, and approached Phillip's house, knocking on the door patiently. After a while, he knocked again; with no response. Williams then heard a noise by the fence near Phillip's house. It sounded almost like something or someone was standing there, but suddenly bolted. Because of this, Williams decided to investigate. If anything, Williams was exceptionally worried that the killer was nearby, waiting to murder Phillip.

From training, Williams knew that if someone tries to avoid the police, the police have the right to chase after that person, since the only reason someone would run from an officer is to avoid guilt. The officer would then be responsible for apprehending the individual by any means besides actually killing them; meaning they would now be able to tread on private property.

"Hey!" the detective hollered as he chased after the sound.

With his flashlight out, Williams trailed along the side of Phillip's house, and eventually the backyard. As he caught up to the run-away, he thought he could see what looked like a scrawny man climbing over the fence.

"PCPD! Get down from the fence!" Williams hollered as he closed in on the scrawny man.

Williams heard shuffling behind him. At the moment, he didn't think anything of it, so he simply kept his pace. Suddenly, there were three flashes, followed by three loud and deafening crashes, which caught his attention. Williams slammed to the ground with a sharp pain in his back. The hits rippled through his body like he was beaten with a hammer; disabling him. When he looked up, he saw that the scrawny man had disappeared behind the fence. Before Williams was able to realize what just happened, he heard someone walking over to him, placing a foot on his back.

"What are you doing in my backyard?" the voice boomed.

Williams could barely breathe under the immense pain in his back. He tried mustering a sentence. "PCPD... who are you..?"

"Dammit..." the man cursed his luck. "I thought you were breaking in or something... I'm not going to jail today..."

Through Williams' radio, a voice could be heard. "Hey Williams, was that you? Are you okay?" the voice inquired.

Williams looked up to see the face of Phillip Hardy above him, who had a pistol in his shaky hand.

"Call the police..." Williams uttered

"I can't!" Phillip shrunk. "They'll lock me up." Phillip caught a glimpse of Williams reaching over to his radio, which he then reacted by pointing the gun to Williams' head. "Don't you dare call for help."

Williams feared for his life, so he held his hands up. Phillip didn't know what to do; he seemed to be pondering his options thoroughly, but he couldn't leave without knowing Williams wouldn't call for backup. Phillip grabbed Williams' handcuffs and placed them around his wrists; he then fled to his house. Williams felt nauseous; his face was in the dirt, and his back ached. Sitting in the dark and lonely silence, a laugh emerged from behind the fence. Williams didn't know what to say with the little energy he had left. Out from behind the fence, someone climbed over, stomping on the dirt below them. Williams could only recognize what appeared to be the feet of the scrawny man, followed by a shovel being dragged behind him. The man's bare legs revealed a cut near his mid-calf region. The cut had been poorly stitched up, almost as if he did it himself.

"Shhh..." the man whispered.

"Hey..." Williams wheezed, but with no reply. He tried warning Phillip, but couldn't scream loud enough.

"I can make your teeth fall out~" the man sang out. "I can make you yell and shout~ La, la, la, la~ There's no need to fuss or pout~ I can turn you inside-out~ I'd find bliss with every cutout~ Don't worry, for you will be knocked-out~ I'll be back for you, there's no doubt~ La, la, la, la~"

The worst part about it was watching the scrawny man walk confidently up through the back door of Phillip's house, having no idea of what was to come next. Williams knew he had to do something about it before it was too late. The handcuff key was in the front pocket of his pants, which was just out of reach; the handcuffs wrapped around Williams' wrists were poorly done. It was obvious that Phillip didn't know what he was doing. The restraints encircled the cuffs of his puffy jacket, which was torn near the shoulders due to the bullets that pierced through. Though tight and uncomfortable, Williams felt like he had the chance to free himself.

The first thing that was on his mind was getting the handcuffs off of his sleeves. This was a delicate procedure; every push in the wrong direction may tighten the restraints. This was a process that took a while but soon proved to aid Williams in his escape. Now that the handcuffs were on his bare wrists, he could try getting his hands out. Since the jacket sleeve was thick, it greatly increased the diameter of the hole; this made it easier for him to slide his hands through. It was still tight though, and Williams was running out of time. With the amount of time it took for him to free himself, he worried about what was happening inside.

Williams was determined though; this killer had to be stopped. Finally, Williams was free at last; a hand was released. He immediately reached over to his radio and tried calling for help.

"Shots fired..." Williams groaned.

The pain in his back was crippling, but he had a choice to make; either he was going to chase after the murderer as an injured officer, or get away and possibly save his own life. Out of these two options, Williams chose to investigate the house. The wounded officer pushed his body up, getting onto his knees, and pulled the ripped jacket from his body, revealing body armor, which had been morphed and twisted due to the bullets from behind. Fortunately, the bullets didn't penetrate Williams' body.

Sergeant Williams grabbed the flashlight that he had dropped beside him; still gleaming through the pitch darkness, now with a gun pulled out and in his other hand. Williams advanced towards the house; the thought of what was to come next almost completely turned him away. If his mission wasn't to protect Phillip, he would just try his best to cover the house to make sure no one left before help arrived.

In extreme circumstances, the human mind will imagine the worst possible scenario; this is exactly the point at which the body will take action to either stand up to the possible danger or run away. At this time,

Williams was wondering if what was behind the walls of this house was something that would haunt him for the rest of his life. As he got closer to the house, he heard a steady pounding coming from inside. Williams slowly made his way up to the back door, where he aimed his pistol at any possible cubby that anyone could hide within.

Entering the house, the pounding became louder. Directly to the left was exactly the source of the sound. On the ground laid the body of Phillip Hardy; above him was what seemed to be a content man slamming the end of his shovel into the skull of Phillip's head. By this time, Phillip's head was a pile of mush, but the man kept smashing; leaving splashes of matter across the floor. Across the room was a lady, petrified and unable to function properly after witnessing the murder of what looked to be her husband.

Williams' heartbeat started to increase, and chills went down his spine. He felt weak and dizzy; a tingling numbness went down his hands and fingers. The man stopped smashing Phillip's skull in, noticing the officer standing there. His face was crooked and unnaturally joyful as if what he was doing didn't affect him at all. It looked to be the face of Owen Reid. Williams started to lose control, his muscles tensed up, and he started to shout whatever came to his mind.

"You killed him, you bastard!" Williams shouted. "Put your hands up! I will shoot you up! Drop the shovel now!"

Owen looked surprised and glad the officer was there. "You came back... to me..?"

Williams tried controlling himself, but his chest hurt. "Drop the shovel now!"

Owen obliged, dropping the shovel to the ground. Williams didn't even notice that Owen had something in his hand, which he had dropped along with the shovel. Two chess pieces clanked to the ground, rolling over to Williams. There was a black bishop and king; both of which startled Williams.

"Now put your hands on your head!" Williams shouted.

Owen frowned. "I couldn't stand the way he shot at you... He was a bad man. This is what happens to bad men."

"I said hands on your head!" Williams repeated.

By this time, there were sirens outside, coming closer to the house. Owen smiled and reached over to the wall. Before Williams could do anything, Owen shut the lights off. Williams looked around the room with his bright flashlight. The man had bolted elsewhere, and now the woman was gone; all that remained was the body that was below him.

"Owen!" Williams screamed. "I'm going to try to warn you now; if you do anything to that woman, you could get really hurt or worse!"

There was no response but a scream from the woman. Williams tried to keep his cool, knowing he needed a collected mind for this extreme situation. He was now concerned that the only thing stopping the killer from harming the woman was him and only him until the other officers could assist. He started to check corners and clear rooms silently.

Myles, Cooper, and Hayden waited nearby for a signal from Williams to come closer. Myles was having a smoke, Hayden was eating a few burritos, and Cooper was messing with his radio. All three officers had been stationed in the same position for quite a while. Myles had just taken his medication; pondering what was about to happen next.

Cooper thought out loud. "Is it just me, or does it feel like this whole case has been bringing some dark cloud over the city?"

Myles shrugged. "That cloud has been there for as long as I've been a cop."

"I mean, like for all the people living here," Cooper added.

Hayden spoke with his mouth full of food. "Everyone is affected by the things we witness. They just don't feel it until they've witnessed it for themselves."

"I wonder how it feels to be one of those victims..." Cooper pondered. "Before they died though. Just the knowledge of knowing you are being hunted down."

Hayden laughed. "You obviously were never bullied as a kid."

At that moment, three loud bangs could be heard from inside the neighborhood. Cooper and Myles looked at each other concerned for where the sound could've came from. Even if it wasn't Williams who made those shots, it could be dangerous if there was a crime being committed while they were around.

Cooper took his radio and spoke into it. "Hey Williams, was that you? Are you okay?" he inquired.

There was no response though, which made the officers very anxious. Cooper and Myles shared a car while Hayden had his own vehicle. Both had their windows rolled down. Myles switched the ignition key, starting it.

Myles turned to Hayden. "I'm going to see where

those bullets came from. Stay here and make sure no one leaves or enters the neighborhood," Myles ordered.

Hayden nodded with no questions asked.

The neighborhood seemed oddly quiet; especially tonight. The ominous silence raised the officer's suspicion as if it knew exactly what was going to happen next. Myles drove at 8 mph, slowly scanning the streets for anything abnormal. He wanted to make sure that if the shots came from somewhere other than Phillip's house they could interfere before it affected the investigation. The drive-by was slow and unfulfilling.

"I don't see anything..." Cooper sighed.

"Don't worry, just keep your eyes peeled," Myles reassured. "If we see something, then we'll step in. If we don't then maybe it was just nothing."

"But Williams didn't answer through the comms," Cooper mentioned.

Myles shrugged. "Who knows, maybe he's on a different channel."

At that moment, a voice came over the radio. "Shots fired..." the voice uttered.

Cooper's eyes opened wide. "That sounded like Williams!"

"Call for backup." Myles composed himself, preparing for the worst possible outcome.

Outside, cop cars circled the house and the neighborhood for anyone on the loose; no one was going to slip past them this time. From the looks of it, Myles and Cooper were setting up for war. Both were strapping each other with vests and equipment, which seemed to be a slight overkill for pistol shots, but they weren't sure what else could be in the house, so they prepared themselves for it. Cooper simply had his sidearm at hand, while Myles carried a shotgun with rubber rounds to make sure that it would take down the target if needed without killing them.

Usually, the officers entering a building would all be lethal, but Myles wanted to stay half lethal; he wanted answers, and he didn't want to kill anyone. Myles took the lead along with a few other cops behind him.

Cooper noticed movement inside; a light flashing around from room to room. "Hey guys, I think I see movement!" he whispered. "I can't get eyes on who it is though."

Myles nodded before turning to his radio. "Hey, Williams? 10-20? There's a whole squad of police making their way towards the house."

A voice came back over the radio. It seemed worried and frightened. "I'm inside the house now. Phillip is 10-45 David, another 10-65, being held captive by the suspect. They're hiding somewhere."

"Are you hurt? You sound like you've been smacked around," Myles observed.

"I was shot," Williams moaned. "Body armor saved my life though. I'm okay; 10-52. The suspect may have a gun with him."

Myles spoke softly. "Come outside; we'll handle it from here. There are some paramedics out here."

Williams obliged, quite relieved to see his colleagues. Now that he knew the situation was under the control of the other officers, he could finally reach the help he needed. With the officers now inside, they started checking every room for movement or anything even remotely close to a person. The first thing they saw as they advanced towards the rear of the house was the man with the smashed head laying on the ground.

"Confirmed 10-45 David," Myles spoke into his radio. "Still no sign of the wife or the suspect." Myles led the group down the dark hallway, slowly making his way through the bedrooms. "Owen!" Myles shouted. "This is the PCPD! If you're in here, I want you to come out with your hands up! Let the girl go! If you don't, this can end up really bad for you!"

Immediately afterward, scratching could be heard from inside the walls.

"Where is that coming from?" an officer looked around.

"There!" Cooper whispered as he pointed towards a bedroom.

Cooper grabbed the door handle, waiting for the other officers to come in. Myles was on the other side of the entrance, waiting for the signal. With one swift kick, the officers flooded the room, covering the room with their flashlights. Still, no one was there. There was still one last place they didn't check, which was the closet. Again, the officers piled up, expecting the worst.

Opening the closet door, the officers blinded Owen, who sat in the fetal position. His right hand was scraping some bloody scissors against the wall; next to him was the woman with a deep cut down her stomach. She was still breathing but barely moving. Owen looked traumatized as anyone would be.

"I didn't do it..." Owen repeated to himself.

"Drop the scissors!" Myles screamed, followed by a dozen officers screaming things that couldn't be understood; talking over each other.

"10-45 Charles," Cooper spoke into his radio. "11-41."

Without showing any sign of fear, Owen started to stand up, clenching the scissors in his hand. The officers started to back away, afraid that the suspect would lunge at them. They warned him to stay back, but he wouldn't respond. That's when Myles fired a rubber slug right into Owen's right mid-torso region, causing Owen to drop to the ground in pain. Officers jumped onto Owen, restraining him immediately.

"10-15," Cooper repeated into the radio. "10-15."

FIFTEEN

REASON

"The woman at the scene, Chloe Hardy, sustained deep lacerations to the stomach with the blade of some dull scissors," Cooper read out to Myles. "After some extensive surgery, Chloe is on her way to recovery. However, Phillip Hardy was found dead at the scene with heavy traumatic brain injury."

Myles felt relieved. "We may have lost another life, but we got the killer. In the process, we saved a life."

Cooper smiled. "All on a day's work, right?"

"Right," Myles nodded. "But now we need to fill in the blanks. I want to really put this case to rest. I could be a patrol officer after this and still be happy. This investigation is like nothing I've ever seen."

Cooper nodded. "It's definitely a start to my career, that's for sure. I'm glad we finally caught someone though. Didn't Williams say he dropped some more chess pieces? Perhaps we could question Owen about the details inside of them."

"Good idea," Myles remarked as he walked to the

other side of the lab to grab the chess pieces. "Which one first?"

"How about..." Cooper thought. "The bishop first?"

Myles agreed, grabbing the bishop with a gloved hand. The first thing that Myles noticed was that the head of the bishop poked out like a pin, but it was held in by a spring. The other thing that was movable was the head of the chess piece, which clicked when turned. It took a few minutes before Myles started to notice it was like a padlock. The only thing was Myles didn't know the code. There were two notches, one on the head and one on the body. When aligned, they would match up perfectly, assuming that it meant zero.

Myles put the chess piece down. "Maybe this one should be saved for last. I'm not sure what the code would be." He then turned to the other chess piece. "If I could connect any dots, I'd say that Philip and the bishop piece have some things in common."

"I think the king piece and Owen make a lot more sense," Cooper admitted.

"How so?" Myles inquired.

"Is it not clear?" Cooper looked at Myles, then back to the king chess piece. "The king calls all the shots. It's the piece that needs to be protected; without it, the game is over. Now that we finally caught Owen, it's all over."

Myles nodded. "At least I hope so. The only reason I could see Phillip as the bishop is that he is the right-hand man of the leader of the group. The thing is that the bishop is the right-hand man of the king, and Owen is the king. Also, why is it that all these pieces have consistently been black chess pieces? Is it inferring that there's some sort of civil dispute between the group members? If so, how does Owen fit into this?"

"I don't know," Cooper shrugged. "Maybe we could just ask him."

Myles messed with the king piece for a while. There were no movable pieces on the outside beside the base, but something shook apart on the inside. It was as if it were a ball bearing going through some sort of maze. The maze inside wasn't long at all, but it still took Myles awhile to actually get through, since technically he was doing it blindly. Near the end, the bearing would fall into a compartment in the base. Once the base was turned, it gave leverage to a release.

Inside was a note; at the top read "Secrets Revealed." Below it was another title that read "bishop code." Under the code was exactly as it was written; a number combination, as if it was a safe. "24-13-23-11_44-13-13-K_43-11-32-11." Myles saw the letter K in the code, simply counting which number K would be in the alphabet. With this code revealed, Myles started to click the bishop like some safe to every number that was presented to him. This combination was exactly what was needed to open it up. Inside was not a note this time, but instead a small rectangular prism.

"What is this suppose to mean?" Myles thought as he inspected the miniature prism.

"Let me see," Cooper asked as he slipped on some gloves of his own.

Cooper examined the glass piece. It was a very light blue color with some sort of small indention on the side of it. The two thought about it, trying to figure out what it could be. A lightbulb seemed to go off in Cooper's head as he looked to a nearby LED lamp. He held the small glass prism up to the light, beaming a shadow on the desk below. The closer the prism was to the light, the larger the engraving became. This small impression in the glass was revealed to be a small number code, much like the code inside the king piece.

"Great thinking!" Myles remarked, amazed that Cooper found out what it meant.

"Learned from the best," Cooper smiled.

Displayed by the prism printed the cipher: "434-142-123-151_161-142-163-163-142-721_111-151." Myles and Cooper both looked at each other, trying to figure out what it meant. They thought of the chance that it could be a date, a word made from numbers; they tried binary, Morse code, everything they could think of to decipher the code. They tried the combination of sentences or words found at the crime scenes; they even checked names and addresses. The two officers sat there trying to think of possibilities but came up with nothing in the end. They knew eventually they were going to have to talk to Owen.

"Ahh, what could this code mean?" Myles articulated furiously.

"There has to be some way to solve it. Possibly Owen himself has the last bit," Cooper suggested.

Myles rubbed his face. "We may not have a choice. We're gonna have to see him soon anyway. If he doesn't give us an answer, we'll just come back to it another time."

Myles reached in his lab coat to pull out a small notepad with some questions written on it; everything else like his cigarettes stayed in his pockets. He put his lab coat on a hanger, keeping a simple gray sweater on for the time being. Cooper followed him out of the laboratory so he wouldn't get locked out with the lights off. Unexpectedly, Myles turned to Cooper; this made Cooper look up in confusion to why they weren't heading to the elevator that just opened up. Myles extended his fist out to Cooper and gave him a genuine smile.

"Nice work with the whole light and prism thing. I would've never guessed that."

Cooper stuttered. "Thanks, Myles." He bumped his fist against his friend's.

"What?" Myles noticed Cooper seemed a little awkward.

"Nothing… I just don't think I've ever seen you smile before," Cooper acknowledged.

"I smile all the time!" Myles was offended. "Like… If there's a joke told to me, I'll laugh."

"I have never seen you laugh," Cooper admitted. "You're just a serious person."

Myles awkwardly tried smiling the whole way to the interrogation wing of the department, even though it was obvious that it was fake; he just wanted to prove a point.

Owen Reid was restrained by a shackle connected to a system of chains bolted to a chair, facing the back wall. Williams and Hayden had just got done getting their two cents out of him, but Myles wanted a little more insight. Cooper and Myles entered the room, sitting behind him in some uncomfortable chairs.

"Afternoon Owen," Myles greeted. "I'm aware Sergeant Williams and Hayden have already spoken to you?"

"Unfortunately," Owen whispered as if he was hiding from someone.

Myles leaned forward. "My partner and I would like

to ask you a few questions if that'd be alright with you." Cooper sat down beside Myles.

Owen turned around in his chair to face the two officers and smiled. A screech came from the leg of the chair as he dragged it across the floor. "Partners? Oh, congratulations. You two look like the cutest couple!"

Myles and Cooper shared an uncomfortable expression, before turning back to Owen. Myles took out his notepad and started asking questions. "Did you murder Jonathan Martly?"

"Yes, no... Yes! No... Yes," Owen nodded. "I didn't 'murder' him. I just killed him because he stabbed my leg. It was self-defense."

"You decapitated the body," Cooper sternly mentioned.

Owen smiled uncomfortably. "He wouldn't stop squirming so I had to do it."

Myles revolved to the next question written down. "You left a chess piece at the crime scene. It was a black pawn with a note inside. What does the note mean?"

"It's simply a date. Did you not understand that from the capital letters?" Owen looked disappointed.

"We got that," Myles pointed out. "What does it mean?"

Owen shrugged. "It's just a date. An upcoming date this month where I planned to have fulfilled my assignment."

"That date passed a long time ago," Myles overemphasized.

"What assignment?" Cooper inquired.

Owen laughed. "To kill all the people I was supposed to kill! Duh!" Owen paused, calming back down. "I'm serious, you two look like such a nice pair!"

Ignoring Owen's statement, Myles went on. "What connections did you have with Jonathan Martly, Erik Vincent, Andrew Sutton, and Phillip Hardy?"

"Well..." Owen put his finger on his chin as he thought about the question. "I did kill them, so I guess we had some connection... We all had such a fun time bonding with each other! We also share a few characteristics. We all have a nose... two ears... two eyes." Owen then paused, followed by a loud and obnoxious guttural laugh. "Sorry... I forgot I cut some of those pieces off..."

Both Myles and Cooper exchanged looks of absolute disgust. Myles cleared his throat before speaking. "You admit to killing Jonathan Martly, Erik Vincent, Andrew Sutton, and Phillip Hardy?"

"Well of course," Owen sighed. "I take pride in my pleasures."

"What did you do to Erik Vincent?" Myles inquired.

Owen smiled joyfully. "That man had such soft, beautiful insides..." His head cocked to one side as he thought of the incident. "I hid in his warehouse until he showed up. He shot at me with his gun, but thankfully I hid behind a bear until he ran out of bullets. Then... I just went up to him and stabbed him... Until the blood stopped coming out."

Myles interrupted him. "Mr. Reid, focus."

"Sorry!" Owen apologized. "He made the animals sad, so I made him join them. I wanted to preserve his body, but I didn't know how to stuff him."

"What does 'Those yond sineth shalt meeteth grievance' mean?" Cooper questioned.

"Those who is't commit sineth shalt meeteth the wrath of death," Owen admitted. "Oh, what a beautiful and poetic way to go out and extinguish the lives of mothers, fathers, sons, daughters, brothers…"

Cooper interrupted Owen's act, moving on to the next question. "What does 'salvation is revenge' mean to you?"

Owen bit his lips. "Exactly as it implies. We are only given forgiveness if we do the work of death. I have surely suffered seeing my little friends go." Owen started to look depressed.

"Why did you leave chess pieces?" Myles intervened.

"I want to give you at least some hint." Owen acted as though that was a stupid question.

Myles stood up partially. "Why did you kill Andrew Sutton, and dress it up as if he did it?"

Owen took a sharp breath through his teeth. "I'm afraid I didn't murder that one."

Cooper shook his head. "We know he didn't commit suicide, and even if he did, he wasn't alone."

Owen shrugged. "He did it himself."

Myles knew he wouldn't say anything about Andrew. "What about the message you left behind from Phillips murder? The numbers 434-142-123-151_161-142-163-163-142-721_111-151. What do they mean? Why did you write them?"

"They were supposed to throw you off," Owen admitted.

"Well, you were obviously planning on being caught," Cooper observed. "Otherwise you wouldn't have left two chess pieces. One of those chess pieces represented you. Your messages can't throw us off anymore now that you're caught."

"Who said you aren't already thrown off by it now?" Owen smirked. "You're asking me what it means because you don't get why I did it. You don't understand anything right now, so you're begging me for answers. I have you wrapped around my finger, and I love it. Nothing makes sense to you right now so anything that comes up would fit into the puzzle. It's easier for me, and harder for you."

Myles started to get irritated. "Where have you been this entire time? You haven't been reported to be at your house. Were you hiding? Do you have another place you could stay?" Myles started to ask questions that weren't on his notepad, feeling angered by how Owen had the high ground.

Owen smiled deviously. "My dear Myles, I simply sleep under your bed at night. Every night before you go to bed, you'll hear a small noise from under your bed. You never really noticed it, but now you will. It's always been me."

"What the..." Myles' eyes opened. "How do you know my name?"

Owen had a blank stare. "You just look like a Myles. That strong chin and those dark blue eyes; it's pretty obvious."

"No, how did you get my name?" Myles had mixed emotions of anxiety and bewilderment.

"Why don't you ask your partner?" Owen turned to Cooper.

Myles was baffled, he turned to Cooper with an unforgiving look. Cooper held up his hands. "I didn't say anything! He's playing with us!"

Myles turned back to Owen. "Do you work with anyone?"

"Yes." Owen started smiling again. "Only the Devil himself."

"That's it, I'm done talking to this guy." Myles got up, and Cooper followed.

Owen just frowned and waved goodbye. "Don't have too much fun together, ya' hear?" In a dynamic change of character, a guttural laugh wretched from his throat as they left the room.

Myles turned to Cooper and took a deep sigh. "He's just messing with us. Everything he says could just be a lie and could lead to further problems with the investigation. The best thing we can do now is to just get him behind bars with the evidence we have now."

"Do we have enough evidence though?" Cooper didn't seem to think PCPD had enough proof; only enough to make assumptions.

Myles crossed his arms. "We have footage from Williams' body cam, which shows Owen butchering Phillip Hardy and his attempt in murdering his wife. We also have him confessing that he killed everyone. That's enough to do something."

"But we don't have all the blanks filled," Cooper countered.

Myles sighed. "We may never be able to fill them in. He might've just made those blanks to make our job harder. We'll keep this investigation going for a few more weeks if we have to. If nothing comes up, then we can assume that it was all Owen's fault and put this case to rest."

SIXTEEN

REVENGE

A few weeks had passed since Phillip Hardy was murdered. Ever since then, things were quiet. The investigation was getting nowhere, giving the officers the impression that it had been resolved. Myles was doing his own tasks, while Cooper did his. Hayden and Williams did the same. The four didn't talk to each other as often after that case. Myles was still signing paperwork he needed to fill out for the investigation against Owen Reid. Meanwhile, Cooper was trying to find a new case, Hayden seemed to just be enjoying his downtime, and Sergeant Williams was working on a new case involving the theft of expensive cars from a dealership.

Myles hadn't seen Cooper for a while now and was hoping he'd show up to work today. He peeked his head into Cooper's office, only to find he still wasn't there. Myles went next door to Sergeant Williams' room.

"Hey, Williams? Have you seen Cooper lately? He hasn't shown up to work for a few days and he's not answering my calls."

Williams shrugged. "Maybe he's just sick. I'm sure there's a reason behind it. Try to see if he's home."

"But he hasn't answered his phone." Myles lingered within Williams' room. "Do you think he just didn't pay his phone bill or something?"

"Could be." Williams kept looking through his paperwork. "Check on him. See if he's alright."

"Fine, but for the period of time that I could've spent doing work, you're going to have to carry my weight," Myles smirked.

"Get out of here before I lose my mind." Williams swatted at Myles to leave.

After working with Cooper for a month or so, Myles really started to enjoy having the extra help. Since the very beginning, Myles was skeptical of having a partner. It was just until now that Myles started to see that this was the best thing that could've happened to him. Cooper was improving every day; becoming a reflection of Myles in a way. Myles was so used to the manner Williams or Hayden acted; bold, experienced, and always did things on their own, much like Myles. Being able to teach Cooper really humbled him in a way. He was able to go back to square one and understand the hardships he used to face. It wasn't only a learning experience for Cooper, but it also taught Myles a few lessons on how to really react to certain situations.

Myles noticed that ever since Cooper became his partner, he started to open up; Myles didn't take things too seriously and brought life to working with his teammates. Because of Cooper, Myles realized that he couldn't keep improving if he didn't start accepting his mistakes. No matter how long one has been working at something, they have to accept that they'll never be perfect at it. As a leader, Myles needed to know this trait, which is exactly why he was given a partner right before he was promoted to Sergeant. This exercise really shows the character change of a naive detective to the officer Myles was at this moment. For that, Myles was thankful.

Being away from Cooper for so long, Myles started to realize how important this exercise was for the two officers. It worried him to know that Cooper was sick enough that he'd be out for a few days. Myles wanted to get him something for his troubles, so he picked up a carbonated drink from the store before he made his way to Cooper's house.

Myles emerged from his car, reminding himself to smile often when Cooper could see it. He was still too stubborn to admit he didn't smile when he was around Cooper. It upset him to see Cooper so surprised to see him smile. He grabbed the carbonated drink from his passenger seat and walked up to Cooper's house.

Myles pulled the screen door open so he could knock, but there was no response. Myles saw that Cooper's car was in the driveway. If he was really sick, he wouldn't be out somewhere, right? Myles tried opening the door, finding that it was unlocked.

"Hello?" Myles hollered. "It's Myles. You in here?"

Myles made his way into the kitchen where he saw Cooper's house phone beeping on the table. The phone recognized that someone was in the room, which activated the system.

"Four new messages," the recorder spoke followed by a beep.

Myles recognized the voice as his own. "Hey Cooper! You've got work today. Just wanted to remind you since you hadn't called in sick or anything. Just wanted to know what was up. I set up a bunch of files that I split with you on the whole Owen investigation. Just wanted to hear from you again. You've been gone for a while buddy, just wondering if you were okay. Call me soon."

"End of message," the phone spoke before a beep ringed; cycling to a new message.

"Hey Cooper! It's your dad!" The Australian accent was even stronger.

"He knows who it is," a woman spoke from the distance. "It says your name on it."

"You never know," Cooper's dad spoke back to what sounded like his mom. "Anywho, we've been waiting to get a call from you for a while. I thought we would see you this Wednesday for an early Thanksgiving reunion. Your brothers are all staying at our place for the time being until you pick up. I know you may be busy with work though so we won't bother you. I just wanted to let you know that we all love you."

A voice came from the distance, sounding like a man with another Australian accent. "Hey! Tell him I love him too!"

"–Oh! And your brother, Oliver, wants you to know he loves you too," racket soon followed in the distance as well. "Ah, your whole family is here and they are all saying that they love ya. Call us when you can. Love ya son!"

"End of message," the phone beeped again, about to cycle to a new message, but Myles stopped it.

"Hey Cooper?" Myles hollered again.

He made his way through the kitchen where he saw a hallway leading towards some bedrooms. "Maybe he is just sleeping?" Myles thought as he made his way down the hall. He looked through every room to check if Cooper was there, but he wasn't. The last door in the hallway was hard to open up. All he could really see was that there were towels under the door, keeping it from opening.

"Cooper?" Myles spoke through the door as he finally pried the door ajar.

The smell coming off the room was sour and musty. It made Myles take a step back before trying to find the source of the smell. As he looked up, he felt his heart sink. Myles didn't know what to do or say; he just felt a strong emotion of denial. His pupils constricted; he felt like he was in an endless tunnel. The sheets were brown and black; rips and holes were cut through the middle where a bulge the size of a body laid. Peering up from under the blanket was the face that Myles recognized as his partner. Maggots purged the body; the skin was marbling and just starting to finish the bloating phase of decomposition. The body had been stabbed more than enough times in the body; most likely as he was asleep.

Myles was too late. The sight of his best friend in such a helpless situation made his heart fill with empathy. He dropped the carbonated drink he had purchased for his beloved friend to the ground; struck by this overwhelming feeling of horror. He felt his eyes water; not because of the overwhelming smell of rancidness, but because he had just lost someone he trusted. Myles backed away towards the kitchen, unable to decide whether he should go for his radio, or just call 911. In the process, he walked passed the dining room, where he saw what appeared to be a white or cream colored pawn sitting on the table.

Some heroes are noticed; some are given the spotlight as the people's heroes. These heroes are able to show their full potential and thrive. Some live on to be able to look back at all they've accomplished and realize their value. Others are short-lived; these heroes may not even be able to hear someone call them heroes.

Cooper taught Myles a valuable lesson. Though Cooper was never able to know how important he was, he made a major impact on the lives of people he knew. His message, legacy, and sacrifice would forever be engraved into the hearts of his friends and family. It pained Myles to know that all it took for him to realize his importance was to lose him forever. He was a hard worker and loved helping people. He had so much potential, and the drive to do it all. Just as he was able to bloom and show off what he knew, he was struck down.

Myles stood next to Hayden, Williams, Anderson and other officers from the PCPD, as well as other police departments around the area. They had finished the ceremony for all officers killed in the line of duty. Though Cooper was in his own home during the time of his death, he was still on duty and was now linked to the streak of deaths involving the killer they were investigating. They were finished with the invocation, followed by prayer, greetings, and scripture readings. The next part of the funeral was the most important part, yet the most difficult. This was the moment when the speakers would then come up to give their prayers out to the family and friends. First, the mayor spoke, then a federal official, followed by family members.

"Such an amazing son..." Cooper's father broke down. "If he can hear me now... All I'd want to tell him is that he made me a proud father..."

The next speaker was Cooper's mother, who cried so long and hard that no one could understand what she was trying to say. She was hurt; broken that someone had taken her baby away from her. The last of the family members were Cooper's older brothers, who had just arrived from across states for an early Thanksgiving reunion. They all came up individually; oldest to youngest.

"I remember when my Mother and Father told me we were gonna have another brother..." the eldest one recalled. "I would always gripe about how we never had enough room because Cooper was coming into the family... Now there's a hole where Cooper left, and there's too much space... That hole is in our hearts. We must remember to keep him there in our hearts to fill that emptiness. He will forever be in our memories and our thoughts."

The next up was the middle child. "Though I may not be the oldest sibling in my family, I felt like I was for my brothers. Cooper was my little brother. Sometimes he'd come to me for lady advise, or if he had any troubles. I wish I could've reacted differently when he said he was going to be an officer of the law. I knew how dangerous it was, and I told him that... I told him how dumb of an idea it was because I didn't want him to get hurt. I should've known he was going to follow his dreams no matter how dangerous it was... I just wish I had the chance to tell him how proud I was of him in becoming the person he always wanted to be..."

Last was the closest brother to Cooper. "I remember the times we use to play catch out in the field behind our house... I remember how amazing it was to finally have a brother that liked sports to hang out with. I remember the times we would prank people coming up to our house on Halloween. I'll miss every time we used to imagine how our lives would be as adults because I know those dreams and stories will now never become a reality. It hurts to know that he won't be my best man at my wedding," he started to break down into tears.

Myles looked down into his hands. Who could've done this? Why would anyone do this? Cooper had done nothing wrong; he was an innocent kid just trying to fulfill his dreams. He was 23 years old; had his whole life ahead of him. Owen Reid was obviously not the only man who was responsible for the deaths. The worst part about it was that there was no message inside the pawn. The message was the pawn itself and spoke a million words. Why would Cooper simply be a pawn? He was obviously worth more than a simple pawn. Perhaps he was on his way to becoming a queen or a rook eventually. The thought of Cooper only being a simple pawn out of many others stung Myles. Did Cooper ever believe in himself? Did Myles ever make it clear that Cooper was worth more than a pawn? Did he treat him as though he was a pawn? A simple obstacle to break through so he could climb the ranking system? The thoughts made Myles sick to his stomach. There was so much Myles could've done better as a leader; a mentor. A fire burned in Myles' heart; a wave of anger started to peer through his better judgment. This pain swelled in his throat, making it harder to breathe.

All that was on his mind was to get revenge.

SEVENTEEN

CRACKED

Myles couldn't bear presenting himself to the crime scene for Cooper's death, so he had to count on Hayden and Williams to take care of the investigation. He still couldn't believe what had happened; things just didn't feel real. The funeral passed, and now Myles was painfully awaiting the results from the lab to come in. It was difficult to focus on the major priorities; he didn't even know the big questions that needed to be asked, like how the killer knew where Cooper lived, or why they did it.

Myles looked over to the spare table in the room he had before Cooper got his own office; he didn't know if he could deal with having another partner after what happened to Cooper. Since he never finished a full year with a recruit, he was going to have to find another to work with. This was supposed to come up in the next few weeks, but Myles was dreading it. He'd be nothing like Cooper was; nothing could compare to him. As he sat in his office, mourning the death of his friend, he heard a knock at the door.

"How're you holding up?" Williams greeted Myles.

Myles perked up, waiting for any news on if they caught the killer. "Did you find anyone?"

Williams nodded slowly. "There's quite a bit of DNA that was found at the crime scene, and it all points to one person."

"Well?" Myles anxiously got out of his chair. "Don't just sit there with the information. Tell me who did it."

Williams held a hand up. "I will, but you have to promise not to go and crack down on the suspect yet. This may be the mastermind behind it all, and we could've been off paced this whole time."

Myles was reluctant but understood. "You know me; I wouldn't do that."

"Good," Williams continued. "Well, there's a clump of hair where we think Cooper pulled from the suspect during the crime; there's dried blood under the fingernails of Cooper's fingers, belonging to the murderer. We think he fought a bit by scratching the murderer before he finally..." Williams paused, trying to be as sensitive as possible. "There's also DNA all over the pawn you found in the kitchen, which belongs to the exact same man as I've mentioned before. Every possible DNA strand in every other place all gives us evidence that there was one person that did this. His name is Dermot Eubanks."

"Dermot Eubanks?" Myles questioned. "What does he have to do with the murders?"

Williams shrugged. "We don't know exactly where he fits in all of this or who he is, but we all feel as though he was the one that wanted them dead. Owen was simply just the one that carried out the murders. Owen had the knowledge of how to kill someone without people finding out, but as soon as he was caught, Dermot had to do it on his own. Since Dermot didn't know what to do most of the time, he got his DNA all over the crime scene."

Myles then started to clench his fists. "Why would he go for Cooper though? Why not me?"

Williams frowned, Myles was clearly miserable over Cooper's death. "Maybe just for intimidation. We don't exactly know yet; that's why Hayden is out to do a little reconnaissance on Dermot. He left a few hours ago, so he should be getting some good insight into what he does." Williams noticed Myles slump down in his seat. "Why don't you go out and get something to eat? If we see anything, we'll be sure to tell you. You should try to relax though and get yourself back into the game. There's still a lot to do. If you'd like, Hayden can do the paperwork that Cooper was in charge of handling so you don't have to work alone."

"Ahh, it's alright. Don't worry about it." Myles got up from his chair and walked towards the door. "I guess all I'll need is some fresh air."

Getting out of the office definitely helped a little with the grief. Myles was able to grab some lunch at a nearby restaurant before he came back to the PCPD. He enjoyed the last remaining minutes of his break inside his car, eating the last of his fries, which he took to-go. While he sat there, he started to ponder the investigation. It was an indiscreet move on the killer's behalf in targeting one of the officers. It was an irrational act too; perhaps the murderer was enraged enough to do such a thing. The biggest problem Myles had with this possibility is how the suspect was even able to know about Cooper. There had to have been some sort of word about him passed around in the area. Another thing that Myles found baffling was how Dermot poorly covered his tracks, so much so, that there was more than enough evidence to place him in jail for life. How was Owen so good at it, but Dermot wasn't? Owen had to be an experienced killer if that were the case.

Myles ate another fry as he pondered the whole situation. It was then that Myles received a call from Hayden.

"Hayden? What's going on?" Myles asked as he picked up his phone.

Hayden sounded stressed. "I've been trying to contact you! Listen, we think we've cracked the case. I'm sending you the coordinates. You won't want to miss this."

"What did you crack? Did you find out who really did it?" Myles inquired.

"Of course!" Hayden continued. "It was Dermot Eubanks the entire time! Dermot is who the Aesthetics refer to as 'The Boss,' and he's been the one handing out assassinations to his own members."

"What?" Myles was mystified. "Why would he do such a thing?"

Hayden shrugged. "He didn't trust them. They knew too much about something we don't quite understand yet. Probably just some drug trade that went wrong like The Sin members were talking about. Once we took out his only assassin, he wanted revenge on us, so he took out Cooper as a warning."

"That bastard!" Myles growled. "Where is he now?"

"He's at a big warehouse doing some business." Hayden's voice got serious. "We're planning on cracking down on him now. I've already got clearance from Anderson. Sergeant Williams is here with a few other cops too. I knew you wouldn't want to miss this..."

"I'll be down there in a solid minute," Myles responded stoically. He was prepared to end this once in for all.

"Once you get here, we'll brief you on the plan," Hayden stated.

"I already knocked and stated our department. I told them we had a warrant for Dermot's arrest, but they didn't open up," Hayden smiled. "I'm glad you could come, Myles. This will surely be something we'll never forget. For the justice of Cooper." Hayden held out his hand to handshake with Myles.

Myles grabbed Hayden's hand firmly and gave him a stone cold expression. "For Cooper."

Hayden continued. "When I knocked and stated our department, I heard them say something about not coming in because they had weapons inside, so be cautious; Body armor is mandatory. I tried to reason with them as much as I could, and it just wasn't happening."

As the officers started to prepare for the raid, other officers monitored the perimeter in case anyone attempted to flee. Hayden carried a shotgun with breaching rounds for doors and entrances, while Williams and Myles armed themselves with compact automatic SMG's for close quarters. All breaching officers were equipped with flash grenades if they felt like it was necessary to use. As ZLEA agents, these officers were trained to take on all kinds of different scenarios including what the swat would normally do.

Sergeant Williams took point at one of the entrances.

Every team had a specific task in breaching the building. They had as far as bolt cutters to C4 explosives if the situation came down to using it. Myles had a hallagan at the ready once Williams gave him the signal. The operation was supposed to be one quick swoop through the warehouse to find and capture Dermot Eubanks.

Williams got the word from the other officers on the perimeter on the building, so he gave a nod to Myles to break the door open. Myles slammed the end of the hallagan in between the frame and the door, pulling it inward and bending the whole metal door apart. It was swift and systematic; Myles turned and kicked the door behind him before getting out of the way to let two officers enter the warehouse.

"Police! Come out with your hands where we can see them!" one of the officers shouted as they entered.

Sergeant Williams took point, covering the corners and entryways as the other officers piled inside. The warehouse was quite massive compared to any in the area; to make sure that the suspect couldn't escape or hide, the team would split up to cover different sections of the warehouse that branched out. Eventually, it seemed to come down to the last stretch of the warehouse.

"Where is everyone?" Myles inquired with his rifle drawn.

"I'm not sure." Williams shrugged. "We'll probably run into them later though." Williams looked at a door that led to a much larger room. "Myles, Hayden, on me. The rest of you, clear out the remaining hallway."

The others nodded as they obeyed the command of the experienced officer. Williams and Myles went to each side of the doorway while Hayden breached. The doorknob wouldn't budge, but it was a wooden door so it would be much easier to break through. Just like in training, Hayden put the end of the shotgun near the inside of the locking system; 45 by 45-degree angle on each side to ensure that whoever was inside wouldn't be shot. A loud shotgun blast rippled through, and Hayden turned to kick the doorway open.

After throwing in a flashbang, Myles and Williams entered the room, making sure to check corners and hiding spots. The large room looked like it had enough room to be a workshop by itself. As they scanned near the end of the room, they spotted what appeared to be a person sitting in a chair facing the wall.

"We got something here!" Williams shouted to Myles and Hayden as he made his way over to the person in the chair.

As Myles got closer, he noticed the man had a sack on his head. He tried to make sure it was clear before he approached the bounded man. In the heat of the moment, Myles aimed his rifle at the man as Williams took the sack off only to reveal an eyeless face with a crooked smile cut into his cheeks from ear to ear.

"It's Dermot Eubanks!" Williams spoke aghast. "But how..?"

At that moment, a deafening shotgun blast rippled through the room, followed by the splash of guts and blood spraying the walls. Myles flinched to some brain matter flying past his face. Williams dropped, dead before he even hit the ground; blood still poured from the headless stump on his shoulders.

"Surprise!" Hayden laughed uncontrollably as he pointed the shotgun towards Myles. "Don't move or I'll have no choice but to make a masterpiece with your brain on the wall!"

Myles looked over to Hayden with disbelief. The fact of the situation didn't fully kick in. "It was… You..? You did this?"

"What do you think?" The expression on Hayden's face turned smug. "How do you feel?"

Myles couldn't think straight. He looked down at his lifeless friend; he noticed the doorway had been blocked with bookshelves and other debris that Hayden moved to keep others from walking in. Blood dripped down from his face; unable to comprehend what had just happened.

"How could you do this..?" Myles cried out.

Hayden seemed to enjoy seeing Myles so defeated like this. "Drop everything you have right in front of you. Try anything funny and I'll make sure you have the worst death of all."

Myles did as he was told, slowly taking out all his equipment and weapons. "I trusted you…" he sobbed as it started to sink in. "I could've saved you!"

"Oh shut your damn mouth, Myles. No one cared, and neither would you. Now turn around and put your hands behind your head," Hayden demanded.

Myles obeyed Hayden, fearing the worst. "How could you do this to him..? Williams taught you everything!"

"How you ask?" Hayden paused to handcuff one of Myles' wrists. "I see you're starting to admire how far I've come." Hayden put the chain around a structural pole in the center of the room before restraining Myles' other hand so he'd be cuffed around the column. "Well my dear boy, let me tell you." Hayden turned Myles so he could face him. "It all started when I met Owen. He was a complete nutcase at first, but I then noticed how important he was. The young man had the drive to kill, and I wasn't about to pass that up. I grew up with him in my teens; he was bullied way too often, so I guided him to salvation. He soon realized how much he loved to kill people that hurt the ones he cared about. I couldn't help it; we worked side by side, just like you and Cooper."

"Murderer!" Myles shouted.

"Murderer? Oh no Myles, you don't seem to understand. Owen did the killing. I just covered his tracks and made sure he didn't get caught." Hayden wiped the hair away from Myles' eyes. "You still don't understand, do you? Let me explain; Erik was the first. I didn't expect him to be the second body to be found, but I was fortunate enough to hide him away until that nuisance Karter took all the fun away. It was Owen's first murder, but I taught him the best I could on how to avoid getting caught. I knew all the tricks and quirks in the system; it was perfect."

Myles' face started to boil with anger. "Traitor!" he spat. "I should've seen this coming!"

Hayden continued. "I suppose Jonathan was next. Poor kid; stabbed in the leg by his second victim," he smirked with no remorse for Jonathan. "I made sure to pick Owen up and get him somewhere safe to patch him up since Jonathan was such a loud screamer. You didn't suspect a thing either."

"You sick bastard!" Myles started to foam from the mouth with rage.

Hayden's tone started becoming more pronounced. "The best part about it all was that I was on the inside, so I knew exactly what you were planning to do next. You came right to me with every little breakthrough you made. I could convince you in a snap and steer you directly off the case. I have to hand it to you, you are a hard one to hide from. As soon as I heard you found some evidence that Owen murdered Erik, I just gave him a simple call and picked him up somewhere nearby. From there I just decided to keep him safe; somewhere hidden. The best part of it all was playing with you; you were like my little toy."

"After all we've been through..?" Myles sniveled.

"I do have to thank you though Myles, I never knew where Andrew lived; I didn't even know if he lived in the area anymore. Thanks to you, you led me right to him. I would've killed him too, but you got in the way. That's not necessarily a bad thing though; I was able to speak to him in the interrogation room so he'd lie to you. It didn't work as according to plan, which didn't matter. You spared his life, and in return, I was able to talk to Andrew one on one. I was able to find out where Dermot had been hiding all this time, and right after, I forced Andrew to take his own life for failing his friends."

Myles lunged forward but was hampered by the pole he was restrained to. "You would've spun me on a completely different track if I hadn't known better!"

"Then there was Phillip," Hayden continued. "I honestly wasn't expecting us to go in on Phillip the day we planned to kill him, but we had no choice. I tried to warn Owen, but he was bloodthirsty. In the process, Phillip almost got Williams out of the way, but sadly missed the head."

"If I wasn't tied down right now, I'd..." Myles paused. "I'd..."

"You know you wouldn't do anything to me," Hayden taunted. "You would never hurt your friend."

Myles tried to break free. "You're no friend! You're a monster!"

"Well, you locked up my killer. It's only fair what I did to Cooper," Hayden's sneered devilishly.

"Shut your mouth!" Myles kicked forward, pushing Hayden to the ground.

Hayden stood slowly and grabbed his shotgun. "Well, that wasn't very nice." Hayden smacked Myles' across the head with the back of the shotgun before continuing. "You shouldn't be so broken up about him anyway. You used him as your little assistant. Tell the truth; you didn't care about him."

"Lies!" Myles screamed.

"I needed a way to get you out of the equation; I needed Cooper, Williams, and you gone so I could focus on the last few I needed to seek my revenge upon. Then, I came up with the most brilliant idea! I was able to smear Dermot's DNA all over Cooper's body so you'd think it was him. It was all a set up from the start. Since I have Dermot's body, I have all the DNA I could ever want; I was able to set up this nice little stage for you."

Myles whimpered. "Why did you kill him..?"

"I needed to start a fire in your heart; otherwise, you wouldn't have fallen for this whole illusion. Your senses would've come to you eventually if I were to tell you Dermot was here and hiding. Cooper would've certainly slapped you out of it too. He didn't put up much of a fight anyways. I just followed him home from work one day and waited for him to fall asleep."

"He was just a kid!" Myles howled.

"A kid that could've blown my cover; now I couldn't have just let that happen, could I? It doesn't really matter now, does it? Now that I spilled the beans and you're tied up here before me. You know, this reminds me of a game I used to play as a kid. I believe you call it chess. You see, there are two types of people in life; there're the competitors and then there're the pieces. You, my dear boy, are a piece, and I am the competitor; Dermot here was my opposition. He had his pieces, and I had mine; do you recognize the similarities? I took out his pieces, so I won. Now that I have won, I don't need you anymore." Hayden reached into his pocket and pulled out a cream-colored king. "Be respectful. I gave you the position of king. Without you, the game would've been lost from the start." He then flicked the chess piece at Myles' face. Since Hayden drove in with Williams, he didn't have a means of escape, so he grabbed the car keys off of Myles' belt.

"You won't get far with this!" Myles spoke in utter rage.

"Sure I will!" Hayden backed away to a corner of the room. "I'll just lie like I always do and tell everyone that I wasn't with you and Williams when entering. It's enough time for me to get to my last problem: Mike. I know exactly where he is and what he's doing. All it takes is one bullet to finish it all."

"I won't let you!" Myles roared.

"What are you going to do? You're handcuffed to a pole." Hayden had reached behind some boxes in the corner and grabbed some bottles with some rags stuffed inside them. "The best part about staging everything is that you always have time to prepare." Hayden walked over to Myles where he grabbed his lighter. "You know, smoking was always bad for your health, Myles. I'd hate to see you go like this. That's why I won't be here to watch," Hayden snickered as he lit the end of the rag on fire.

Myles' heart started to race; as if it wasn't already. He started to fidget with his cuffs. At that moment, a voice could be heard from the radio. "There's nothing here... Sergeant Williams? Does anyone have anything?"

Hayden knew he was running out of time. "I really hoped you enjoyed solving my puzzles. Sorry it had to end this way, old friend. You should've stuck to forensics." Hayden backed away from Myles slowly before smashing the Molotov against the ground, igniting the floor below him. Through the smoke and the flames, Myles could only see the twisted smile on Hayden's face as he walked back to a set of ladders leading up to the roof.

Myles screamed and hollered trying to get the attention of the other officers, but was unfortunately inaudible. Myles knew that if he didn't think of something quick, he was going to burn alive. Myles always had a spare handcuff key in his belt, but his belt was in the pile next to Williams' body. It might've been out of reach for a lot of people, but due to the length of Myles' legs, he was able to kick over the belt if he laid down and stretched his body out as far as he could. The fire was starting to clash with the other flammable objects in the room, spiraling out of control, but Myles was determined to escape.

Myles reached deep into his belt pocket to pull out his spare handcuff key which almost fell out when pulling it away from the flame. The anxiety was rising as Myles struggled to free himself as the fire grew higher. The air in the room grew thinner with each breath he took, but alas, Myles freed himself from the restraints.

EIGHTEEN

Myles crawled on his hands and knees, avoiding the smolder so he could muster enough oxygen near the ground to get out. He reached over to Sergeant William's body and grabbed his car keys before heading for the same ladder Hayden exited. He watched as the plastic king piece melted onto the floor near the fire. Scalding metal panels plummeted onto Myles' back, causing the detective to shriek in pain as he stood up. The jacket he wore scorched into orange and red flames. As the fire slowly engulfed him, Myles frantically ripped off excess clothing, including his bulletproof vest to save his own life.

The smoke grew worse as he tried making his way past the rubble that fell apart from the ceiling. As he desperately grasped the ladder handles, the metal bars burned Myles' hands, leaving red marks on the palms. Baring the pain from it all, Myles managed to climb onto the roof of the burning building; it was a relief to finally breathe fresh air. Time was running out though, and Myles needed to prevent another life from being taken. Myles ran across the roof of the warehouse, making his way to another side of the building where a ladder dropped off into the parking lot.

A few officers came over to see the condition Myles was in. "What's going on here?"

"Where did Hayden go?" Myles demanded.

"He left in his vehicle," the officer answered. "I guess he was going to get something?"

"You didn't stop him?" Myles shook his head. "Where did he head off to?"

"In that dire—" The officer's pointed in a direction, but Myles ran off before they had a chance to finish.

Sprinting off towards Sergeant Williams' cruiser, Myles knew there was no time to lose; he raced the electric car recklessly onto the road. He expected to shift in this vehicle but was pleasantly surprised. Without hesitation, Myles grabbed the mic off from the radio and started speaking.

"Officer 516 of PCPD; Code 2, on pursuit of a 10851 2025 black classic special, heading northbound. Driver of the vehicle is Officer 163. Code 9 is needed." Myles then turned his sirens and lights on before changing frequency. "There's an 11-71 at 6800 Burlwood Drive. Evacuate officers and suppress 11-71."

Myles changed to the frequency he knew his radio was on in his car. He wanted to know if any locations were listed from Hayden. Down the road, Myles could spot his car casually driving down the road. As soon as Hayden saw the flashing lights, he booked it, grinding into the gears of the transmission.

"It's over Hayden," Myles spoke as he followed Hayden down the narrow street. "Pull over."

"How did you..." Hayden grumbled. "Come on

Myles, you can't tell me that with a car like this, I'd just hand myself over would you?"

Hayden turned into streets without warning in an attempt to throw Myles off, forcefully changing gears. The electric car Myles was in had powerful torque so it could keep up just as long as Hayden didn't reach full horsepower. Hayden made a sharp turn pushing in the clutch and pulling the parking brake, making the back tires slide with the vehicle. With ease, Hayden let off the parking brake and clutch, making a perfect drift across the street. Myles struggled, trying to make a complete turn without drifting.

"Hydraulic parking brake, V8 supercharger, come on Myles, you can't tell me you didn't plan on using the car for this purpose did you?" Hayden pulled onto a busy intersection, making his way to a service road.

Myles turned to his radio "Code 2! Heading Southbound onto highway 155!"

"You're really starting to get on my nerves," Hayden hissed.

Hayden repeated the drifting process, turning onto the service road. Myles couldn't afford to lose ground, so he too used the parking brake on the cruiser, making it drift across the turn. The parking brake started to seize, producing a burning smell. It took a while for Hayden to get back up to speed, which was perfect for the electric car to catch up. Myles tried nudging the back of Hayden's vehicle with the vehicle's push bumper, but Hayden tried a few dangerous maneuvers to get away.

The next idea Myles tried was knocking into the rear corner of Hayden's vehicle to make him spin out. It was dangerous but effective. As an officer that knew these tricks, Hayden protected these weak areas from being hit.

"Get off my ass!" Hayden cursed as he grabbed a pistol from the side door of the car.

Myles started gaining up on the right side of Hayden's vehicle, but before he could get close, Hayden fired as many rounds as he could at the driver's side of the cruiser. One of the bullets ricocheted off the A-pillar of the vehicle and smashed through Myles' abdomen.

"Gah!" Myles screamed as excruciating pain shot up his back.

Most of the bullets cracked the windshield, making it considerably difficult to see. In one quick motion, Hayden made a complete U-turn onto incoming traffic on the highway. Myles struggled to turn with one hand on the steering wheel, and the other under his chest, where blood gushed out.

"Code 2!" Myles repeated. "Pursuit on a 10851 onto highway 155 westbound..."

Myles flinched at every car that flew by his vehicle, traveling inches past him. At this point, Myles was starting to lose distance on Hayden since the V8 was so fast on the road. Myles could identify flashing lights in the distance on the service road; it was a relief to know that some assistance was on its way.

"You're not going to stop me from finishing my job!" Hayden snapped.

Hayden leaned out from the car window, starting to fire a couple shots behind him at Myles. The smug smirk on his face changed as he turned back around to see an oncoming car heading straight for him. Hayden slid back into his vehicle, trying to swerve out of the way, but because the vehicle was moving so fast, Hayden lost control and started to roll over violently, smashing into other cars in the process. Myles tried to avoid the cluster of collisions ahead, but wasn't able to do so fast enough; he clipped into the corner of another vehicle, stopping both cars right in their tracks.

Myles was dazed and confused from the head-on collision. Fortunately, the airbags deployed properly, saving his life. His arm was stuck inside the steering wheel, deformed and awkwardly disfigured. For other reasons, Myles was bleeding profusely from his abdomen. What an ugly sight; metal bits and pieces were scattered across the street. Hayden's car was upside down, crumpled up like a squished aluminum can. Myles tried walking up to the trashed vehicle; civilians got out of their cars to watch what was happening. The bleeding officer stumbled over his own feet as he walked along the skid marks on the highway; behind the mass of mangled cars were more oncoming traffic, which soon came to a complete halt.

Myles' head was excruciating due to the collision, and his arm was out of place and swollen. He fell to his knees, crawling to see if Hayden was still alive. To his surprise, Hayden still had his hands on the wheel; blood streaking down from his face and nose. The airbags gave him a soft cushion to rest on. Hayden looked ahead, imagining the car was still right-side up.

"What... did... you... do..?" Hayden's voice was deep and serious, yet calm. "You... You ruined it all."

All petrol vehicles at the time of the 2025 special was created with bladders in the gas canisters in case there was a leak. In a crash like this, the bladder could crumple and seep flammable gas. Myles was aware of this and wanted to get Hayden out as quickly as possible.

"Give me your hand!" Myles reached for Hayden's arm.

Hayden groaned as he looked down to his shattered legs. "Mercy..? I don't want your damn mercy. I want to see you suffocate. I want to see you perish."

Myles tried crawling closer inside the upside-down vehicle. "You need to trust me!"

"Leave. Now," Hayden demanded

"Get out of the vehicle!" Myles tone turned more and more desperate as time ran out.

"I can't!" Hayden burst with pain. "My legs are stuck!"

"Give me your arm!" Myles reached. "I'll pull you out myself! With or without your legs!"

Hayden smiled. "If I go out... I'm taking you with me..."

Hayden forcefully grabbed Myles' broken arm and pulled him into the cab of the car. Myles painfully struggled to break free, knowing there wasn't much time left. Oil and gas leaked onto the concrete below them, creating a dark purple, green, and blue reflection. The fuel started to flow near the steaming engine, getting closer and closer. Myles pulled with all of his might until eventually, Hayden lost his grip and let go.

Hayden gasped out. The look on his face was filled with mixed emotion. For a moment, Myles saw the faintest glimmer of repent as if he still depended on Myles to save him. This tormented Hayden; in the last moments of his life, Hayden knew that he had no one.

"No!" Myles shouted, seeing the fuel ignite, consuming the car in flames.

Myles held his arm up due to the extreme heat radiating from the car. Hayden started to fall apart, bursting into an uncontrollable laughter. Failure and misfortune was all he ever knew in his life. The inferno slowly devoured him, and the laughter soon became agonizing shrieks of anguish.

Myles dragged himself back, propping his body against the street rails. He grew tired and dizzy; around him was a puddle of blood, which only grew as he waited. All he could see in the distance was flashing lights and officers running around, trying to handle the situation. Everything seemed to go in slow motion. It felt better to close his eyes after a while, even though the people surrounding Myles attempted to make him stay conscious. He saw a distant white light that warmed him like no other. He felt safe; he felt happy.

Yearning nothing more than to rest his body, he fell under a spell of full comfort; he desired the feeling to sleep for a while. This urge to doze off only became more compelling as he laid there.

Laying there with his face to the warm sun gave him hope. Perhaps this sun was the light all along? Or was it something more that he was never able to understand? Amongst the destruction around him, he found a sort of peace within himself.

Eager to find out what this feeling was, Myles wanted to be left alone. He didn't want others to find him, or to rescue him. He was ready for what was to come, but though he was ready, he was afraid of the truth to be displayed before him.

Sorrowful for his friends and family, Myles had one last wish to see them before the inevitable. He couldn't move, couldn't speak, couldn't hear much at all.

"..."

"Is this how this ends? What will my mother think?" He contemplated the outcome in his mind. "Would it matter now that I have no one? That's not true. I must fight this; I must stay strong."

"Surely by now, there had to be someone that has noticed me here," Myles thought. Cooper, Hayden, Williams; they were all taken from him. What was to come of him in the future?

"..."

Gazing through the smoke and wreckage, anyone would want to leave this all behind, but Myles didn't. He saw through it all and knew he wanted to stay. He had to stay strong.

Only those with a sound mind could truly find their way out of this, but did Myles have this trait? After losing and being betrayed by the one he loved, did he have the strength to go on like this?

Neglected like an abandoned child, could he afford to lose it all? With all he loved gone, would he go missing? Astray from right or wrong, he went with a choice. He had to take a chance and make sure to stick to it.

Even the bravest and best heroes fall eventually. There's nothing that could be done for the ones that put their life on the line for the safety of others; even if it's just one life.

Myles could feel himself drift through darkness into a much brighter subsection. There he looked across and saw a figure emerge from the glow. Blinded by the light, only a silhouette could be seen, which took form as a much larger being. Myles didn't know what to say; he just reached up to the being as it slowly kneeled down to him as if he were a child. Only then did he recognize the face of this being.

Myles' eyes watered, and his hands went over his mouth in shock. "Dad…" he whispered, trying to piece together the right words to speak.

"I'm so proud of you," Myles' father smiled. "So brave; so strong."

Though Myles' face was wet from the tears, a smile grew across his face. He understood where he was now. There was a wave of peace and happiness that flowed through Myles' body, now understanding that the world had to keep revolving; life went on.

Myles' father put his hand on his son's shoulder. "I've seen your successes, and I've seen your hardships. I've seen you grow and I've seen you bloom. You've lost and you've fallen, but out of everything you've been through, you still stand strong; you still care and you'll always have a purpose in the lives of the people you've met."

Myles wiped his face gently. "I only wanted to be like you… Mom would always tell me stories about you. She'd always tell me how great of a father you were…"

His father frowned. "The biggest regret I have is not being able to be there for you when you needed me… Though in the end, it made you stronger; you faced life alone. You still have so much to learn."

Myles looked down. There was a long silence as he thought of what to say. "I miss you Dad…"

"I miss you too Myles… I couldn't have asked for anything better of you. You're everything I hoped you'd be," his father smiled. "You're still young though; you have to keep going. You still have so much to live for, and you still have a chance! You still need to take care of your mother."

"But I don't want to leave you… It's hard to go on without you…" Myles looked up to the man he admired most.

Myles' father shook his head. "I never had the decision to decide, but you do. Use it to help and make the world a better place. Don't let this be the end of a great thing; use this as a way to grow."

Myles was still twisted between two sides. A part of him knew there was more out there that he could do or help with, while the other side wanted to stay in this infinite bliss. The world started to twist and turn as the silhouette of his father started to evaporate.

"No…" Myles started to desperately reach for his dad, but his hand futilely phased through him. "Don't make me leave…"

Color started to blossom, and Myles started to come back to the world he knew before. Everything was so surreal, it was almost like it was all a dream. Now that he was back from this alternate world, it felt like a dream within a dream; nothing felt the same. Something felt out of place. He opened his eyes, finding himself laying beside a charred car. The street was dead, and there was no sign of movement. Everything felt stagnant.

"Wha..?" Myles sat up straight, looking around him. "Where am..?"

From inside the car, someone started to crawl out. Smoke poured out from the car as a man emerged. The man's skin was charred and melted, his clothing was as crisp as a twig, and the smell was worse than anything he had ever come across. The man crawled towards

Myles and held him down. Myles was too afraid to do anything, and for some reason, he couldn't move.

The man smiled down at Myles. "See you in hell..."

A loud bang came from the door beside Myles, reviving him from his sleep. Breathing fast and loud, Myles looked around the room he was in, disoriented and dizzy.

"Help!" Myles screamed, unknown to his surroundings.

"Hey, it's alright; it's okay." A voice came from the door, putting a hand on Myles' arm.

The air made Myles groggy, and the room was dimly lit. He was surprised to see Karter above him, reassuring him with a gentle pat on the shoulder.

"It's alright pal, it's just me," Karter smiled.

"Where am I?" Myles looked around, starting to hear a beep come from his right.

"You're in a hospital. You were taken to the emergency room after they found you next to a burning car. You were bleeding pretty bad... It's a miracle you're still alive!" Karter gave Myles a gentle hug.

Myles didn't know what to say. He was dressed in a mint green gown and had IV catheters in his arm. He looked under the gown to find his whole torso patched up and bandaged.

"Oh! I brought you these." Karter pulled out a bouquet of flowers and put them in the vase near Myles' table.

"Thanks, Karter, they'd bring a lot of color to the room," Myles smiled as he tried to get up.

"Hey, hey, be careful!" Karter helped Myles lay back down. "You're still really weak. You just went through surgery yesterday. They had to dig out a bullet fragment that was too close to an artery. It scrambled up your insides a little when it went in."

"I feel sore as hell," Myles groaned. "Where am I again?"

Karter laughed. "Maybe you should rest a little more. Anesthesia usually makes you feel dizzy for a little bit after you wake up. I'll be right beside you the whole time."

"How long have you been here?" Myles inquired.

"I just came back from lunch actually. I've been here ever since I heard you were going through the operating room though."

"As long as I have someone to talk to while I'm here, I'm sure I'll be fine." Myles smiled. "Seriously, where am I?"

NINETEEN

SPLINT

Case closed; at least what was believed to be known about the case was closed. The halt in murders led the detectives, or... the detective... to believe that it had been resolved. The whole event up to when Myles stripped his equipment off was recorded on his body camera and was used in court against the two criminals, Owen Reid, and Hayden Vower. Owen admitted to all convictions and was currently pending on execution for the murder of Jonathan Martly, Erik Vincent, and Phillip Hardy; as for his partner, Hayden, the deaths of Andrew Sutton, Dermot Eubanks, Cooper Alcorn, and Tyler Williams were all placed under his name. Unfortunately enough, Hayden was never rescued from the burning car and died from his critical burns. After 45 minutes of attempting to rescue Hayden from the burning car with his legs attached, he was beyond help. Though a number of people were involved in the wreck, no one else was killed; only a few bystanders suffered minor injuries.

Prior to the court date of Owen Reid, PCPD found

more supporting evidence that proves Hayden and Owen guilty of a number of first-degree murders. A few weeks after the death of officer Tyler Williams and Hayden Vower, a funeral was arranged, which Myles Connor attended and spoke about his career alongside his friends. Recently, director Martin Anderson assigned Myles Connor a new partner named Haiden Patterson, who is believed to start acquaintance in the next month or so. Myles is not looking forward to a new partner, especially one with a name similar to Hayden.

By now, everything had settled down; to Myles, it settled down a bit too much. He sat in his office, writing illegible and unrecognizable sentences with his left hand; his dominant hand was supported by a wrap that went around his shoulder in a splint. He contemplated the horrible deaths of his friends; all of which, he believed he could've done something to prevent.

It was unnaturally silent in his office this afternoon. He was used to being interrupted by Williams, Cooper, or Hayden; now it was just empty. To the left and right of Myles' room was vacant; the little corner on that floor was always the best for him because his friends were right next to him like a neighborhood. Now Myles had nothing but work to do; the uncompleted assignments his friends were tasked with were handed down to other officers in the station that were willing to take it. Now all Myles had to do was to move on. He was used to working with a team, but now that they were gone, it made everything a lot more difficult. Myles wanted to stay positive though; he was glad he still had his mother, who he'd visit every weekend, and his friend Karter, whom he tried to hang out with any time he could. He was just settling into the day when he heard a knock at the door.

"Come in." Myles looked up.

An officer peaked his head through the open doorway. He didn't seem very familiar; Myles inferred he was from one of the lower floors. "I've got someone here that wants to talk to you about the investigation. His name is Mike Robertson; would you like for him to come in?"

"Sure thing," Myles waved him in. "I've got nothing better to do," though obviously, he was up to his neck in paperwork.

The face of a certain loudmouth came through the doorway. The same one that Myles, Cooper, and Williams first questioned for information on the murder of Jonathan. Though he wasn't a lot of help before, he was still a person who would flap his jaws about anything.

"Mike." Myles tried smiling but came off as intimidating as always. "What brings you here? Grab a seat."

Mike sat down in the seat opposite from Myles; he seemed solemn and somber. "Well, I'm sure you know about everything. I don't know whether you put this whole investigation to rest or not, but I really want to give more. I heard about how you saved my life. If it wasn't for you, Hayden would've gotten his revenge one way or another."

Myles' face turned grave and the atmosphere in the room changed drastically. "I'm afraid there's nothing else that needs to be answered. I don't suppose you have everything we need, do you? I'm honestly quite surprised you know the name, Hayden."

Mike sighed. "I have my reasons. I don't have much of a gang anymore; everyone involved was completely cut loose. I'm not sure what will happen to The Aesthetics, but I'm worried. I'm sure things will get better, but we is really sensitive now over the loss of our brothers. I know you feel the same about your people."

Myles frowned. "Yeah... It's been pretty hard here too. We're one of the same. I'm all ears; tell what you must."

"Right," Mike started. "Have you looked into Hayden's history recently?"

Myles shook his head. "Not very recent, but I know he was clean up until this crime."

Mike sat back, taking a deep breath in. "He had a hard life growing up. I'd have empathy for the guy if he wasn't such a psycho."

"I knew he was an orphan," Myles stated. "That's all I really know about his past. What does this have to do with the investigation?"

"You see, Hayden grew up in a bad part of town. That town is where he met me, Dermot, Phillip, Andrew, Eric, and Jonathan. At the time, we was just a bunch of kids; we didn't know what we was getting ourselves into. We did things just because it's what the real gangsters did. Once we got older and found out more about living life dangerous, we didn't like it as much, but we stuck together since the beginning; that is... for me and the others. Hayden was a weird one; he didn't fit in, but he tried as best as he could."

Myles still didn't get where this was going. "Alright? What else do you know?"

"People saw Hayden as a real freak, y'know? He had that huge scar on his head, and no one really knew about it. Some say that he got it when he was barely old enough to go to school. His mom and dad fought a lot; the dad was an alcoholic. One night, he heard fighting coming from his parents' bedroom; he peeked through the little crack in the door to see his dad holding a gun up to his mom's head. He saw his dad murder his mom right in front of him. As any kid would feel, he was scared shitless. 'What did you do to Mommy?' he screamed as he walked up to his dad. That's when his father put the gun up to his own son's head and pulled the trigger. Some say it was just luck that gave him the chance to live; others say the dad looked away as he pulled the trigger so the bullet simply grazed his head. It's a terrible thing to think about it. Right afterward, the dad shot himself in the head."

Myles was horrified; he never knew Hayden went through something like that. Hayden just reassured Myles it was from an accident from his childhood.

Mike continued. "Hayden woke up after the death of his parents; all he did was walk out of his house and down the street to his neighbors; acting like nothing happened with blood running down the side of his head."

"Are you saying that this whole time, Hayden killed because of a traumatic experience he had as a child?" Myles supposed.

"I'm getting to that," Mike shook his head. "I think it's just one of the reasons why he'd go that far. It wasn't the reason he went after us though. Since he was seen as a freak, we used him; he thought it was just a way for him to fit in, but we were just getting a laugh out of him. It got worse once he started getting older..."

"What happened?" Myles inquired.

"We started to get physical with Hayden during the last days we saw him. It was bullying; no matter how much we abused him, manipulated him, put him through peer pressure, he just started laughing along with us... Like harder than we were laughing. We'd beat his knees in with a baseball bat, strangle him, hit him on the side of the head with racquets or shovels, and even slice him up with the end of a razor blade. Sometimes, he'd be the only one laughing, and he'd be doing it for hours like some lunatic. We didn't like it, so we planned a day we would really teach him a lesson. One afternoon, I believe it was the 28th of October, we skipped school with him. We took him over to some storm drain that was open and threw him in. Before he was able to get out, we slid the metal cover over. He was trapped, and no one was around to help him; we just left him there until someone found him. Later that day, it rained pretty hard; so bad that the whole streets were flooded, and the storm drains were overflowing. There was no way Hayden would've survived, so we just kept it as that; we didn't tell nobody. We never saw him again, and we were glad of it."

Myles could see what impact this would make on a teenager. "He didn't die though, so what happened between you and him?"

"We heard he went to some private school after that, but that was just rumors; we still didn't believe he was actually still walking. That wasn't until we got the news that Jonathan was murdered. We simply thought Erik was in hiding so he wasn't responding; in reality, Hayden was coming for us. Some of us didn't believe it, but some of us did. Phillip slept with a shotgun next to him every night. He probably shot that one cop because he thought it was Hayden."

"Why didn't you tell us this when we were questioning you?" Myles knew that if it weren't for this, Cooper, Williams, Hayden, Dermot, Phillip, and Andrew would've still been alive.

"We didn't know exactly if it was true," Mike confessed. "We knew it was him, but we couldn't prove anything. Plus, we thought if we says anything, we'd be next. We just hid from him; hid from all the awful, terrible things we did to him. We should've known he'd find us eventually. I'm just glad I know I'm safe. I'm the last of the group that survived, and it's all thanks to you."

Myles felt a sort of hatred for Mike, but he reminded himself it was all in the past; they were only kids. Myles couldn't arrest Mike because it was many years ago, and there was little to no evidence that supported this claim. Nevertheless, Myles felt some empathy for Mike; like Mike, Myles also survived this whole maze of an investigation.

Myles sighed. "At least we now know the reason why Hayden did it. The investigation is closed now though, so there's nothing I could add."

Mike shook his head. "I'm just saying this to make you relax. Consider it a way to finally move on from what has happened. Maybe Hayden's ultimate torture for me was to take my family away from me. It's certainly keeping me up at night."

"You kidding?" Myles was irritated. "This is going to keep me up every night for the rest of my life! I still have nightmares ever since Hayden died. He was looking for a way out, but I stopped him from getting revenge. For that, he hated me for it… I just still can't believe he'd just snap like that. I knew him for so long. I trusted him... at least I thought I could."

Mike looked down to his feet. "I'm sorry for your friends. I thought this could help you move on in your life, but it didn't help a thing."

Myles realized he wasn't being grateful. "It's alright. I appreciate knowing more about Hayden so I could put my suspicion to rest. I'm just going to ask one thing from you; if we happen to cross paths again, we will not speak of this. I don't want your typical mouth flapping, you hear me."

Mike nodded as he slowly stood up. As he walked to the door, he paused, thinking about what Myles had agreed to do. "You know, getting over something doesn't mean running away from it. It will just make things a lot harder for yourself," Mike spoke before leaving.

Myles rubbed his face with his hands and thought to himself. It was a lot to take in all at once. Though what Hayden did was wrong, he had his reasons for what he didzon. His definition of justice was corrupted by his rancorous background. If Hayden was led down a better path, Cooper and Williams would have still been able to see their families. Myles could have made it through to Hayden when they were once companions; was it all just an act to hide the trauma that manifested itself into Hayden's thoughts? Running away from these thoughts created this unnatural need to seek vengeance; perhaps this is what Mike was referring to before he left. Whatever the case may be, this slip cost the lives of many. Myles thought he'd go mad as Hayden did if he were to continue pondering these thoughts. So many possible outcomes, and out of all of them, Myles managed to lose everyone.

Special Thanks To

Ethan Nguyen

Lori McClanahan

Peggy Chrusciaki

Marty Cain

Angela Blehm

Katie Adams

Doug Poteet

You; The Reader

For Making This Possible

Printed in the United States
By Bookmasters